"I think you're terrified of letting me into your life."

Jack's mouth tightened. "In case you haven't noticed, you *are* in my life. I didn't have much choice in the matter, you barged right in and took over."

"And you hate that," Abby replied.

"Maybe I resented it at first."

"And now?"

"This argument is going nowhere." He cut her off. "Your mother wanted to know what my intentions are toward you."

"And what did you tell her?" Abby's smooth brow furrowed.

"I told her we were just friends." Jack took a deep breath and released it slowly. "I'm not sure she believed me."

Jack was no longer sure he believed it himself, either.

Dear Reader,

Your best bet for coping with April showers is to run—not walk—to your favorite retail outlet and check out this month's lineup. We'd like to highlight popular author Laurie Paige and her new miniseries SEVEN DEVILS. Laurie writes, "On my way to a writers' conference in Denver, I spotted the Seven Devils Mountains. This had to be checked out! Sure enough, the rugged, fascinating land proved to be ideal for a bunch of orphans who'd been demanding that their stories be told." You won't want to miss *Showdown!*, the second book in the series, which is about a barmaid and a sheriff destined for love!

Gina Wilkins dazzles us with *Conflict of Interest,* the second book in THE McCLOUDS OF MISSISSIPPI series, which deals with the combustible chemistry between a beautiful literary agent and her ruggedly handsome and reclusive author. Can they have some fun without love taking over the relationship? Don't miss Marilyn Pappano's *The Trouble with Josh,* which features a breast cancer survivor who decides to take life by storm and make the most of everything—but she never counts on sexy cowboy Josh Rawlins coming into the mix.

In Peggy Webb's *The Mona Lucy,* a meddling but well-meaning mother attempts to play Cupid to her son and a beautiful artist who is painting her portrait. Karen Rose Smith brings us *Expecting the CEO's Baby,* an adorable tale about a mix-up at the fertility clinic and a marriage of convenience between two strangers. And in Lisette Belisle's *His Pretend Wife,* an accident throws an ex-con and an ex-debutante together, making them discover that rather than enemies, they just might be soul mates!

As you can see, we have a variety of stories for our readers, which explore the essentials—life, love and family. Stay tuned next month for six more top picks from Special Edition!

Sincerely,

Karen Taylor Richman
Senior Editor

Please address questions and book requests to:
Silhouette Reader Service
U.S.: 3010 Walden Ave., P.O. Box 1325, Buffalo, NY 14269
Canadian: P.O. Box 609, Fort Erie, Ont. L2A 5X3

His Pretend Wife

LISETTE BELISLE

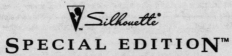

SPECIAL EDITION™

Published by Silhouette Books

America's Publisher of Contemporary Romance

With special thanks to my editor Stephanie Maurer
and my friends at SRWA who share the dream.

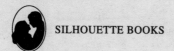 SILHOUETTE BOOKS

ISBN 0-373-24536-X

HIS PRETEND WIFE

Copyright © 2003 by Lisette Belisle

This edition published by arrangement with Harlequin Books S.A.

Visit Silhouette at www.eHarlequin.com

Printed in U.S.A.

Books by Lisette Belisle

Silhouette Special Edition

Just Jessie #1134
Her Sister's Secret Son #1403
The Wedding Bargain #1446
His Pretend Wife #1536

LISETTE BELISLE

believes in putting everything into whatever she does, whether it's a nursing career, motherhood or writing. While balancing a sense of practicality with a streak of adventure, she applies that dedication in creating stories of people overcoming the odds. Her message is clear—believe in yourself, and believe in love. She is the founder and past president of the Saratoga chapter of Romance Writers of America. Canadian-born, she grew up in New Hampshire and currently lives in upstate New York with her engineer husband, Frank.

She'd love to hear from her readers. She can be reached at P.O. Box 1166, Ballston Lake, NY 12019.

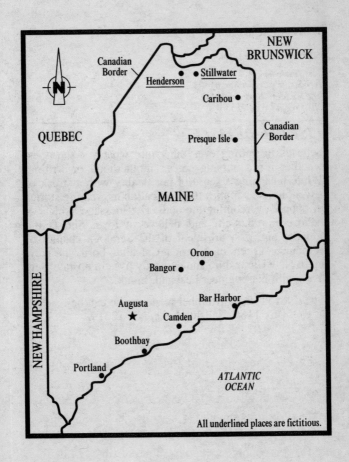

Chapter One

No one would miss him.

Jack Slade had never felt so alone. He stared up at a small patch of deep-blue sky surrounded by snow-capped pine trees. The sky felt closer. He was climbing to meet it, but something weighed him down.

He wasn't ready to go yet.

How odd to discover he wanted to live, just as he was about to die. He started to laugh, but wound up choking. God, it hurt to breathe. That had him worried. He'd probably cracked a couple of ribs, but that didn't explain the knife-like pain in his chest. Exposed to the bitter cold, he wondered how long he could survive.

Hours?

Would he see another dawn?

The ache in his left leg was gone; at least that part of his body felt blessedly numb.

Deep in the northern Maine pine woods, Jack was miles from anywhere. Earlier, he'd cut down a section of hardwood. When the rest of the logging crew left, he'd stayed on, hoping to get out one more load before quitting for the day. He'd almost finished when a doe crossed his path.

Startled, he'd swerved to avoid it. For one long sickening moment, the log skidder had started to tip. Jack tried to right it, but the track was uneven, covered in a thin layer of ice. The huge mechanical beast went into a slow roll, finally landing on its side and pinning him underneath.

Luckily a foot of packed snow had cushioned his fall, but there were rocks buried beneath. He'd struck his head and had been knocked out for a while. Now he lay trapped.

Ironically, he'd survived street gangs, a rough-and-tumble youth and even a spell in prison—only to wind up in a primitive forest in Maine. He'd read somewhere that logging, filled with physical hardships and risks, rated third from the bottom when it came to optimum occupations.

Maybe he should have aimed higher....

Abby Pierce lingered in her office at the Pierce Sawmill. Her assistant had gone home. The old post-and-beam building was eerily silent. No screaming saws, no grinding trucks loading and unloading outside in the lumberyard. No rumbling masculine voices—one voice in particular, calling her ''Miss

Abigail,'' its owner taunting her with his sinfully blue eyes and a hard enigmatic smile, undoubtedly intended to put her in her place—wherever that was.

Abby glanced at the clock on the wall. Jack Slade was late, probably working—or stopped off at the diner flirting with a pretty waitress. For some reason, women were drawn to his dangerous edge.

But not Abby.

With an impatient sigh, she closed the payroll files. Jack hadn't come in to pick up his paycheck, and she was tired of waiting for him.

It was New Year's Eve—a time for shedding the past and looking to the future with new resolve. Lately, Abby's life seemed caught in a holding pattern. She had a date with Seth Powers that evening. She should go home and change into the midnight-blue dress she'd purchased for the occasion, but something held her here. She couldn't leave.

With a frown of irritation, Abby admitted the reason behind her unease—Jack Slade hadn't checked in yet. Why should she care? Why indeed?

Abby rose hastily, dismissing the notion that Jack, with his dark good looks and devil-may-care attitude, could mean anything more to her than a thorn in her side. Like bad news, he'd arrived out of the blue, claiming her brother owed him a favor. Drew had given him a job, and she'd rued the day ever since. Was it only two months ago?

It seemed longer.

Nothing in Abby's sheltered life could have prepared her for a man like Jack Slade. He was everything nice girls like her had been taught to avoid.

Abby stared out the window overlooking the lumberyard and watched the daylight fade to dusk. No matter how hard she tried, she couldn't ignore the parking space where Jack's logging truck should be. His motorcycle took up the space.

Running her hands up and down her arms, she felt chilled and weary. And worried. Jack could be hurt, or lost in the woods. It happened to even the most experienced loggers, and Jack hadn't been around that long. Nevertheless, he wouldn't thank her for sending out a search party simply because he was a couple of hours late.

Abby glanced up at the sky. Night was falling, and with it, the temperature. That settled it.

Taking a deep breath, she walked into her brother's office. "Have you got a minute?"

Drew looked up from the pile of paperwork spread out on his desk. "I thought you'd left by now. What's up?"

"It's Jack. All the other men have checked in, but there's no sign of him."

Drew leaned back in his chair. "He's probably just getting in a last load for the day. I wouldn't worry about Jack, he can take care of himself."

Abby had heard that before, it was little comfort to her now. "But it will be dark soon." Afraid to reveal her personal interest, she admitted, "I know it doesn't make any sense. I just have this bad feeling."

He raised an eyebrow. "About Jack?"

She ignored the amusement in his voice. Naturally, Drew was aware of their mutual dislike. Jack was Drew's friend—not hers. *Never* hers. From the first moment they'd met, it had been hate at first sight. Abby couldn't hide her disapproval and Jack had responded with male derision. To this day, their working relationship remained awkward.

"Please," she said, putting her reservations aside, "can you just check on him? Or send someone up there?"

"All right." Drew reached for the topical map—an aerial view of the section of forest where the logging site was located. "He should be just about here." He circled a dot on the side of a mountain. "I'll go have a look around."

Abby looked at the map, aware of how easy it would be to get lost. How long could a man survive out there?

"I'll come with you," she said on impulse, unwilling to be left behind where she would worry. About Jack. The knowledge curled around her heart and squeezed.

Half an hour later, they found the logging site. Jack's truck stood parked by the side of the road. There was no sign of Jack. Abby felt a shiver of dread.

The mountain stood before them; a rough logging track cut a path upwards. Huge black rocks penetrated the pure white snowdrifts. Drew shouted Jack's name into the silence. No answer. Only the wind whispering through the stand of towering pine trees. By now, a pale white winter moon rode high, frozen in black space.

Drew handed Abby a flashlight. ''Here, you'll need this. Stay close. I don't want you getting lost.''

Abby nodded. She didn't need to be reminded.

The climb was rough going, icy in spots. The surrounding forest was thick. Some winter branches were bare. In the moonlight, the shadows lengthened, darting in and out. The woods seemed to close in around Abby, bearing her down as the steep climb stole her breath.

She felt a stitch in her side. Ignoring the dull pain, she kept climbing. Then she saw the fallen skidder, the bright yellow flash of metallic paint against the frozen white landscape.

''Drew, look over there, to the left.''

Drew shouted back, ''Any sign of Jack?''

Abby shook her head. ''No, it's too dark.''

''Don't worry. If he's here, we'll find him.''

''He might have wandered off,'' she said. For all his outer toughness, Jack was an inexperienced woodsman.

Abby walked closer to the fallen skidder. Under the twisted metal, a form took shape, broad shoulders in a buffalo plaid wool jacket.

''Jack,'' she whispered, struck by the ominous silence all around her. Her heart stopped. Then, started again in a new erratic rhythm.

Abby rushed up the incline. She slipped once, but struggled to her feet and continued on. With Drew behind her, she was the first one to reach Jack. Removing one glove, she sank down on her knees beside him, and searched for a pulse in his throat. She held her breath—until she felt a slow but steady throb beating under her fingertips.

Jack was so still. Wedged between the ground and a heavy metal strip, only his head and shoulders were exposed. His hair gleamed black against the snow. His face was pale, his lips blue. A bloody, inch-long gash stood out against his wide brow. His thick eyelashes fanned out over high cheekbones.

He was frowning.

Typical.

Abby had rarely seen him smile.

"He's alive?" Drew asked, the words clipped and taut.

"Yes," she murmured, finding her voice.

Drew released a harsh breath. "Looks like he's been here for a while. Good thing the snow provided some insulation to keep him from freezing."

Abby's eyes filmed with tears of relief. "Thank God."

Jack Slade was alive, he was going to be all right. She refused to consider anything else.

"Don't move him. We don't know how badly he's hurt." Drew stood up, his cell phone in hand. "But by the look of things, he'll need an airlift to the nearest medical center. I'll give Seth a call, so he can get right on it."

Abby nodded. In addition to being the local sheriff, Seth Powers was a good man to have around in any emergency.

While Drew called for help, Abby turned her attention back to Jack. She brushed his hair away from his brow, surprised at the soft silky texture. Everything about Jack Slade seemed so hard.

Half-conscious, Jack felt a woman's soft, soothing touch. With only distant youthful memories of his grandmother, he wondered if he'd died and gone to heaven. He opened his eyes and encountered hazel eyes rimmed in gold. He knew the woman leaning over him.

One thing for certain—he wasn't in heaven! Not with Abigail Pierce on hand to torment him.

"Abigail." He tried to tell her to go away and leave him alone. But the words remained locked in his throat. Why did she have to plague him now?

She leaned closer—her breath warm against his face. "Please, lie still. You're safe."

"Safe?" he said in confusion. How could that be when he was lying battered and half-frozen with his leg crushed and a black sky falling on him? Maybe this was all a nightmare, and he would wake up any minute....

"Drew's here with me, he's calling for help. They should be on the way." Her face went all soft. Jack stared, mesmerized, as she continued. "A few more hours and you would have frozen. Where does it hurt?"

Trying to lift his head, he sank back and shook off a wave of dizziness. He focused on her voice. "Everything's numb, but I think my arm's broken." He swallowed hard. "My left leg's bad. I know it."

"Just hang on. Help is on the way."

Jack shook his head. There was no one to turn to—except Abigail Pierce. And she wasn't even a friend.

The story of Jack's life. He'd been betrayed one too many times to trust easily, and Abigail was no exception to his rule. However, faced with no alternative, he had to make do with her.

"My leg's pinned under the metal bar. I can't move it, I can't feel it anymore." His eyes trapped hers. "It's probably pretty mangled." His voice dropped a notch as he struggled for words. "Don't let them take it off."

"Jack, no—" Abby paled, her eyes wide and shocked. "You can't know if it's that bad."

"I know," he said, grimly reminded of that terrifying moment. He'd felt the metal tear through flesh and bone—a white-hot pain. "Promise?"

Silently, she nodded.

He shivered. "It's so damned cold."

To Jack's surprise, Abby removed her long wool coat, then draped it across his shoulders.

"What about you?" he asked, wary of being on the receiving end of her kindness. There was always a price.

"This is fine. I'm wearing a thick sweater." She placed her gloved hand on top of his head, as if to keep the heat in his body.

Like a slow tide, he felt some of her warmth seep into him. Afraid to rely on that one small charitable act, he closed his eyes, shutting her out.

"Jack!" Aware of the added risk of hypothermia, Abby panicked. "You can't go to sleep. Drew's organizing a crew to come and lift this thing." She kept talking, saying anything that came to mind to keep him awake. "Seth put in a call to get an emergency evacuation helicopter to fly up here and airlift you to a hospital.''

''Where?'' he murmured after a long moment.

''A downstate facility where they have experience in dealing with injuries like yours.'' When he said nothing, she leaned closer. ''Jack, do you have family, anyone I can call?''

He opened his eyes, shocking her with a vivid blue stare. She could see intense pain in the depths. He looked so vulnerable. ''There's no one.''

''There must be someone,'' she said desperately.

His eyes flickered over her face. ''There was just Gran and me. And she's gone.''

''I'm sorry.''

His eyes narrowed. ''Why?''

She sighed. ''I don't know. I just am.'' *Everyone should have someone.* She didn't voice the words.

Help finally arrived—the sheriff and some loggers and a local ambulance manned by trained volunteers. Abby stepped aside to give them room. After a quick evaluation, they placed an oxygen mask over Jack's face.

Abby felt helpless while a crew of men worked to free Jack. Through it all, the sheriff clipped out instructions, creating order out of chaos. Strong and reliable, Seth was in his element in any minor or major emergency. Abby knew she'd ceased to exist for him in that moment.

It was nothing new.

Duty always came first with Seth—a noble trait, but Abby wasn't sure she could settle for his steady, stable but unexciting courtship. Would their marriage be like that? Seth charging off—a knight in shining armor to enforce the law and rescue anyone who needed him—while she waited for him to remember she existed? Was it selfish to want more attention, more devotion? More *passion?*

At length, the dim overhead clatter of the rescue helicopter grew closer until the roar was upon them. A blinding white light beamed down, piercing the night and illuminating the accident scene.

Abby glanced up, shielding her eyes with her hand.

The helicopter dipped low, hovering. An amplified voice called down, ''We're going to land in a field nearby. That's as close as we can get. Hang on. We'll be right there.''

It seemed to take forever but was actually less than fifteen minutes before the medical rescue team reached Jack.

Mindless of the cold, Abby helped them wrap Jack in warm blankets. When a medic cut at the denim fabric encasing his leg, she caught a brief glimpse of the injury to his upper thigh. Swallowing hard as the bile rose in her throat, she averted her gaze from the sight of torn flesh and bone. Nevertheless, even with her inexperienced eye, Abby had seen enough. Jack hadn't exaggerated the damage to his leg. He had every reason to worry about losing it.

Horrified by the realization, Abby didn't notice her brother had come to stand by her side until Drew handed her the coat she'd loaned Jack earlier.

''You look frozen,'' Drew said.

Dressed in a thick wool sweater and slacks, Abby

didn't feel the cold. Nevertheless, she slipped her arms into the sleeves of her gray coat. The quilted silk lining felt warm from Jack's body heat.

"Thanks," she whispered, her lips trembling.

Drew gazed at her with concern as he asked, "You okay?" Sometimes she felt he understood her better than she did herself.

Abby laughed shakily, wondering if she was losing her mind. "Jack's the one with the problem."

He had looked so helpless—at the mercy of fate. From what she knew of Jack's troubled past, life had dealt him more than one blow. Would he survive this latest one?

Drew tried to bolster her. "He's in rough shape, but it could be worse. He may not realize it right now, but he owes you his life."

"I didn't do anything." Abby refused to accept any responsibility for Jack's life.

That might open up a set of emotions she'd tried to deny since the first day she met him. From that day on, she'd been bombarded by feelings that threatened to disrupt her ordinary, orderly life. But wasn't change the reason she'd moved back to Henderson? Feeling restless and generally dissatisfied with her life, she'd hoped Seth was the answer.

Seth was safe.

Jack was the unknown.

"You sent out the alarm," Drew pointed out, a question in his eyes when her silence lengthened. "No one else knew Jack was missing."

She had known. In some secret part of her, Abby was aware of Jack's every move. She knew when he arrived at work and when he left—to the minute. She dreaded and craved each new encounter. God! How had she let herself get drawn in by his brooding good looks and the masculine taunt in his bitter blue eyes? Today, she'd glimpsed a flash of vulnerability in Jack Slade—something she'd never expected to see beneath the tough exterior.

Abby wasn't sure how much time had elapsed before a medic gave the order, ''Okay, let's get him out of here.''

A new urgency gripped her.

The rescue squad had set up flares to light the way back down; the mountain looked on fire. The paramedics bundled Jack onto a stretcher. Since the helicopter had landed in the nearby field, a couple of men had to carry him down the steep mountain path, a slow tedious process.

Following in their wake, Abby felt Jack getting further away from her, breaking that small but very real connection she'd felt earlier when they were alone and he'd asked directly for her help. Then the others had arrived.

He didn't need her.

Falling back, she breathed easier. Someone else would look after Jack Slade. Not Abby. He was terribly hurt, perhaps critically, but there was nothing she could do for him. Thank goodness, there were professionals on hand who knew how to deal with his life-threatening trauma.

Despite all the rationalizing, she wanted to cry when the men loaded the stretcher bearing Jack onto the helicopter feet first. They'd wrapped him in a blanket and splinted his left arm. No one had dared touch his left leg, except to gently wrap the brutally torn flesh in sterile gauze.

As if pulled by an invisible thread, Abby took a step. "Someone should go with him," she said to one of the medics climbing on board.

The man glanced back at her. "There's room for one more, but only the immediate family is allowed."

"Please, wait." Abby swallowed hard.

She had no personal connection to Jack. They weren't even friends, and she preferred it that way. Nevertheless, she'd made a promise—one she found impossible to break or ignore. He'd asked her to save his leg, and she'd agreed.

He was counting on her.

How could she ignore that?

Faced with that grave responsibility, a small lie hovered on her lips. She couldn't let Jack go alone. He was unconscious. Who would look after him?

Though it was the last thing Abby wanted to do, some deep instinct compelled her to claim an attachment to Jack Slade with the words, "I'm his wife."

Chapter Two

His wife.

Abby pursed her lips, regretting the impulse the moment the words spilled from her mouth. However, once spoken, she couldn't take the false statement back. With a few rash ill-considered words uttered in desperation, she'd claimed Jack Slade. How could she? In any case, she had little time to reconsider or come up with an alternative plan.

Preparing for liftoff, the pilot turned on the motor. The engine's roar drowned out all thought. The helicopter blades spun, circling in a wide arc, churning up a thick white cloud of snow. Abby felt swallowed up in it. A few ice crystals struck her face.

She'd blocked out her brother's presence.

Drew tried to stop her. He'd obviously heard her claim that she was Jack's wife. He grabbed her arm, raising his voice above the motor. "Abby, this is insane. What are you doing? You can't just pretend you're married to Jack."

"He's unconscious." Abby pulled free and took another step closer to the waiting helicopter. "He can't go alone, not in his condition. How will he cope when he gets to the hospital? Someone has to go with him."

"But not you. Jack means nothing to you."

Abby squared her shoulders. "That's not the point. He needs someone. There is no one else."

Drew's mouth tightened with disapproval. He searched her eyes for a long moment before releasing her. "All right, but God help you when Seth finds out."

She shook her head. More than anything in the world, Abby wanted to feel truly connected to some place. Someone. Perhaps that someone was Seth Powers. And yet, she found herself saying, "Seth doesn't own me."

Drew said dryly, "Try telling him that."

With a shiver of acknowledgment, Abby turned away from the warning in Drew's eyes. When the paramedic reached down to give her a hand, she climbed on board the helicopter then quickly found a seat.

The sharp scent of antiseptic stung her eyes. A paramedic inserted an intravenous into the back of Jack's hand, while asking, "How was he when you found him?"

"He said he was cold."

"Did he recognize you?"

"Yes, he did."

The man nodded, he was middle-aged with a kind face and thick eyebrows that shadowed his eyes. "That's a good sign."

"Jack will be okay?" She needed some reassurance, something to hang on to.

"We're doing all we can. The thing is to get him to a hospital where the doctors can deal with his injuries. The nearest medical center is a good distance. So, hang on."

"Yes, of course." Fastening her seat belt, Abby took a deep breath to steady her nerves.

With the weight of her promise heavy on her conscience, she glanced at Jack. He lay still as death, and she prayed that he would live, that he would be whole.

She reached for his hand. "Hang on, Jack."

Jack would never have asked for her help if he weren't desperate. She'd seen it in his eyes.

From the moment they'd met, he'd seemed unapproachable, his hard eyes challenging her and a cynical edge creeping into his smile when he greeted her with a few terse words. He'd asked to see Drew. Abby hadn't been able to see past his black leather jacket and motorcycle, but her brother had greeted Jack like an old friend. They'd met in prison—which did little to improve Abby's opinion.

At the time, Jack had seemed so alien to all that was familiar. Since then, she'd never been able to shake that feeling of impending chaos. He threatened her secure world, adding to her concerns for her brother who was trying to rebuild his life after serving time in prison for violating federal safety code regulations.

Abby frowned, recalling that tumultuous time.

At the trial, Drew had pleaded innocent to the charge. However, he'd admitted to repairing a faulty gas tank valve instead of replacing it with a new one. That one error in judgment had caused an explosion at the family-operated migrant campground. Thankfully, no lives were lost, but the list of serious injuries and property damage was long. A jury had found Drew guilty, and the judge had thrown the book at him. Sentenced to five years in prison, Drew's punishment hadn't ended there. Everyone had turned their backs on him, his family had closed down their extensive farming and logging interests and left Henderson. Only Abby had remained loyal.

Three months ago, she'd come back to Henderson when Drew was released. Determined to atone for his mistakes, he'd reopened the sawmill and Abby had joined him. She'd invested both her time and money in the effort. Thus, she hadn't been pleased when Jack Slade—an ex-con—turned up at the sawmill looking for a job. He was part of Drew's past, a threat to the future.

Now, Abby leaned her head back with a sigh, admitting that she resented Jack's presence for more personal reasons.

According to Drew, Jack Slade was an innocent man, wrongly imprisoned for a crime he didn't commit. Perhaps that part was true—but when Jack looked at Abby, there was nothing innocent about him.

For the first time in her life, she'd seen naked hunger in a man's eyes. When she'd shrunk from Jack, his expression had quickly turned to derision. She'd been running away from him ever since.

Not that Jack noticed, she thought with a sad smile. He was obviously a loner.

Abby understood isolation.

She was the product of a small backwoods town and an exclusive boarding-school education. Separated from everyone and everything she loved best, she'd spent her childhood not knowing where she belonged. She'd been searching ever since.

Maybe Jack was searching too.

How odd to think they might have something in common—anything at all. Unwilling to grasp the implication, Abby glanced out the window.

Buffeted by a strong north wind, the helicopter lifted off the ground. The roar of the motor drowned out her thoughts. Flying into the clouds, she looked down at the ground below where Seth had joined her brother. Both men grew smaller and smaller as the helicopter gained altitude.

The downstate medical center was miles away; the trip seemed to take forever. In reality, it was less than two hours. Gradually, the city lights came closer until they were sweeping down onto the hospital roof, a flat rectangle that seemed too small to land on. Abby held her breath until the helicopter touched down with a jolt. It had reached its destination, but Abby's journey was just beginning. Once the copter was anchored securely, she climbed down. She wrapped her coat around her, thankful for its warmth against the bitter cold and recalling how she'd shared it with Jack. Was he warm now?

An experienced hospital triage team took over.

After they exchanged a few hurried words with the rescue crew, a sense of urgency filled their faces. They sped Jack away. With very little experience of trauma, illness or hospitals, Abby struggled to keep up as Jack was whisked inside the building then down a labyrinth of corridors to an elevator. Doors opened, people rushed down hallways.

In the emergency unit, a nurse took over. "What's his condition?"

While someone responded, the paramedic who had assisted Abby on the helicopter patted her shoulder. "He'll make it. I have to go. Good luck."

Abby caught her breath. She wanted to cling to him, he was the only familiar face among so many strangers. "Thank you," she whispered. She didn't even know his name, but he'd been kind.

When Jack disappeared through another set of swinging doors, the nurse barred her way. "I'm sorry. You'll have to wait until the doctor has examined him. Admissions will want to speak to you. Someone will let you know if there's any change in the patient's condition."

"And please try not to worry," she added as an afterthought.

Abby wondered how many times the emergency-room nurse had to repeat those words in the course of a routine twenty-four hours. In any case, they did little to reassure Abby.

Feeling cut off, she retraced her steps and found the waiting room. A few tired decorations stood as a reminder that it was only six days after Christmas. She'd spent the holiday with Drew and his wife, Olivia. Abby wondered how Jack had spent the day.

The admissions desk was partitioned behind a wall with only a small window connecting it to the outside world.

Abby tapped on the glass to get someone's attention. "I'd like some information," she said when a nurse turned up.

The window slid open a few inches. "Weren't you with the patient they just flew in from Henderson?"

Abby gripped the edge of the counter. "How is he?"

To Abby's mounting frustration, the nurse answered indirectly. "We're doing all we can." She handed over a brown envelope. "Your husband's valuables are in here. You can take them home with you."

Feeling like a fraud, Abby took the thick envelope, then slipped it unopened into her coat pocket. "Can I see him?"

"One of the doctors will speak to you directly. In the meantime, I need some information."

Abby volunteered Jack's name, age, address, insurance information. She knew all those from his employment records at the sawmill. Allergies? None— that she knew of. Another line remained—next of kin.

Jack didn't have any family to notify. Struck by the absolute aloneness of this man, Abby stared at the blank space, then took a deep breath. Gripping the pen, her hand shook as she penned in the name Abby Slade.

The black letters looked stark, a little thin and wobbly, nevertheless, the indelible ink couldn't be erased. Releasing her breath, Abby dropped the pen on the counter.

To her relief, the receptionist gave the signature only a cursory glance. "We'll let you know if there's any change."

The glass partition slid shut.

Completely cut off, Abby struggled with the urge to call the woman back and confess the deception. But then, she remembered. *Jack.* She'd promised to look after him. As the lies mounted, that was the only truth that mattered.

Abby bit her lip, buried her guilt and turned away. The thought of legal repercussions did cross her mind briefly; however, she dismissed the concern, refusing to let second thoughts deter her from helping Jack. Pretending to be his wife was a bit extreme by any standards, but as his self-appointed representative, she could see no other way to guarantee that he received the right treatment.

The waiting room was crowded.

A child was crying plaintively.

An elderly couple clung to each other.

Some teenagers talked too loudly in the hushed room.

Avoiding them, Abby bought a cup of coffee from a machine. Fortunately, she carried her wallet in her pocket. She found an empty chair. When she sipped the coffee, she spilled a few drops on her coat. Glancing down, she realized her hand was still shaking. She carefully set the cup down on a table.

Untouched, the coffee grew cold.

What was taking so long?

To distract herself, Abby watched a woman crocheting a pale-yellow wool scarf. Repeatedly, the ball of yarn rolled off the woman's lap and onto the floor. Abby retrieved it twice before realizing the woman was apparently caught up in some inner turmoil and didn't care. Abby wished she knew how to offer comfort. But the words remained locked inside. When the ball of yarn fell a third time, Abby looked away.

"Mrs. Slade?" The doctor had to repeat it twice.

Abby jumped. He was speaking to her. "Yes?"

He was frowning—not a good sign. "You came in with Jack Slade?" He looked down at some notes. "It says here you're his wife?"

Abby couldn't find the words to deny the connection to Jack. She nodded. And so, the web of lies grew.

And grew.

The doctor pinned her with a look that had her bracing her spine for bad news. "I don't need to tell you he's in pretty rough shape." Not mincing his words, the doctor listed Jack's injuries—a minor concussion, a broken arm, a couple of cracked ribs and a punctured lung, some possible internal injuries and spinal swelling. "We won't know the extent until we take X-rays and run more tests."

With each added word, Abby's head spun. This was much worse than she'd feared. Poor Jack. Gradually, she became aware of what the doctor *wasn't* telling her. "But what about the injury to Jack's leg?"

The doctor wouldn't meet her eyes. "We have to get him stabilized first. Then we'll see."

Abby took a fortifying breath. "Please, just tell me."

"I'll be frank. We'll do what we can, but I can't perform miracles. We may have to amputate."

Abby gasped. "But you can't do that!"

He argued, "We may not have a choice."

Choices.

Abby tried to find words to persuade him. "But I know Jack. He would never give you permission."

"He's unconscious. In cases like this, we'll need your permission as his next of kin."

She clenched her hands and slid them into her coat pockets. "I won't sign anything. I want Jack to have the best surgeon available. I don't care what it costs."

She could afford to pay the medical bills. More than likely, Jack would resent being an object of her charity. Well, he could just go ahead and hate her. At least, he would be alive and kicking—hopefully, with both legs.

The doctor offered no encouragement. "Flying someone up from Boston might take more time than we've got."

"I'll accept full responsibility."

He frowned. "If you're determined to do this, I won't try to talk you out of it. I suppose you want to see him. I'm warning you, he's not a pretty sight. The next hours are critical. If he's going to make it, he's

going to need you to stand by him with every ounce
of courage you can muster.''

Courage.

Abby wasn't sure she qualified in that department.
She'd never been tested, never had to fight for anything she wanted. Or anyone. Of course, the doctor
was assuming she was married to Jack, which meant
she must be in love with him. Thank goodness she
wasn't in love with the man! A woman would have
to be out of her mind to love Jack Slade, or very
reckless. And Abby was neither.

Apparently, taking her silence as consent, the doctor ushered Abby into the treatment room. There, she
was shocked to find a hospital chaplain giving Jack
the last rites.

Thus, while a medical team worked over Jack's
damaged body, the chaplain prayed for his soul. And
Abby prayed for a miracle.

The lights glared bright and white; the room was
green and sterile. A nurse said sympathetically, ''I'm
sure your husband can feel your presence. He's semi-
conscious, but if you speak to him, he might hear
you.''

Feeling awkward, Abby leaned closer. ''Jack, it's
me—Abby.'' When she repeated the words, he turned
his head, his eyelids fluttered. His face was ashen, the
gash on his forehead stood out in stark relief. ''You're
going to get well,'' she whispered, touching her lips
to his, as if to breathe more life into him. ''Don't give
up.''

When he made no response, she held his hand. It
was hard and calloused. And warm. Despite his grave

injuries, his spirit was strong. She clung to that thought, wanting to believe it was true. From what she knew about Jack, he was no quitter. But would he recover from this latest blow? Even if he survived his injuries, the doctor didn't hold out much hope when it came to saving Jack's leg.

Jack clung to something.

Hope?

He wasn't sure where he was. He didn't remember many details of the accident. There were brief flashes of a helicopter ride; everything else was a blur. The pain was intense. He drifted in and out of consciousness, unaware of what was real and what was not, haunted by the fear that his leg had vanished into thin air. He couldn't walk, couldn't run. Voices penetrated the thick fog.

He opened his eyes, surprised to see his bedside surrounded by faceless shapes. Someone was praying over him. How many times did he have to repent? In truth, he was only guilty of making wrong choices and trusting the wrong people. Was he bitter? Yes. Nevertheless, the prayers soothed his soul and made him wish he had a life to live over.

Given a chance, he'd do so many things differently.

His grandmother had done her best to teach him right from wrong. She'd even insisted he serve time as an altar boy. Somehow, according to Gran, that was supposed to keep him out of trouble. It worked— but only after he'd beaten up the bully on the block who teased him for wearing a dress—standard altar-boy issue. After he won the boy's respect, the other kids had left him alone, which suited Jack. He didn't need friends, he didn't need anyone.

Anyone who believed otherwise was a fool.

So much for the past. He didn't have much of a future. He frowned when someone took his hand. Someone feminine clasped him firmly, palm to palm. He tried to hold on, returning the pressure, and felt the flutter of a pulse racing against his thumb. His own heart jumped in his chest. Reality started to fade. The room and its occupants receded, everything turned gray. More prayers. Jack couldn't make out the words. But he recognized one voice.

Abigail.

He struggled to grasp her presence. Had she been around earlier? He was hurt, possibly dying. Why couldn't she leave him in peace?

Then, incredibly, he felt her lips against his—as soft as he'd imagined. In his dreams.

So, this was a dream. He welcomed her presence because everything around was cold and dark and empty. On the inside, he was burning up, a white-hot pain knifed through him with each breath.

"Please, Jack, don't give up." That voice pulled him back from the brink. Her soft words penetrated the cloud of pain, making it almost bearable. "Everything's going to be all right."

He wanted to believe her.

His hand clenched around something soft and feminine; he wanted to hold on and never let go.

Time lost its meaning.

Hours later, while the rest of the world prepared to celebrate the arrival of a brand-new year, Abby sat alone with Jack in the intensive care unit where he was recovering after surgery. The doctors had dealt with the worst of his injuries—all but his leg—and he was breathing better.

Abby was still recovering from the shock of what she'd done—she'd lied, more than once, claiming to be Jack's wife. Amazingly, no one had questioned her. Now, she was alone—with Jack. She'd never felt more frightened in her life.

She should call someone back home. No doubt, her brother was waiting for news of Jack. Somehow Abby couldn't deal with all the questions. Not yet. A day of reckoning would come soon enough. She wondered how much Jack would remember—if anything.

She'd used her fake status to insist the doctors delay surgery on Jack's leg until the following day. A top surgeon was flying up from Boston. Jack still wasn't out of danger. She desperately wanted him to get well. That was the only real part of this whole charade.

A new year was about to ring in. In the holiday spirit, a nurse brought Abby some pastries and mock champagne—fizzy apple juice. "I know it's difficult. But you'll need your strength. You really should eat something."

"Thank you." Abby obeyed, unable to recall when she'd last eaten. All that was normal seemed unreal.

Jack's accident had wiped away everyday considerations. How odd to realize that life could change and rearrange itself in a heartbeat. From the moment

Abby had realized Jack was missing, nothing had been the same.

The nurse injected some medication into Jack's intravenous and adjusted the drip. "If it's any comfort, the whole staff is pulling for both of you."

"That's very kind of you. Please thank everyone."

"Have you been married long?"

Unable to hide her growing discomfort, Abby blushed. "Not very long."

"You must be very much in love with him."

Abby wanted to shout a denial, but she couldn't bring herself to burst the young woman's romantic bubble. "How can you tell?"

"It shows." The nurse smiled. "If you're planning to spend the night, the chair's comfortable. You'll find an extra pillow and some blankets in the closet." Before she left, she added, "Oh, I almost forgot—your brother called."

That startled Abby. "What did you tell him?"

"That Jack's current condition is stable."

"Oh."

Abby had no idea how she was going to explain her erratic behavior to her family. In addition to her parents, she had three brothers. Drew would understand. He wasn't exactly known for his caution. In fact, his impulsiveness had gotten him into trouble a time or two. However, claiming a relationship to an unconscious man would be considered extreme even by Drew's standards.

There was simply no explanation for her rash decision to embark on a rescue mission that included masquerading as Jack's wife. After the nurse left,

Abby sipped mock champagne from the paper cup, wondering if she was losing her mind.

The midnight hour came.

A flurry of hushed well-wishers out in the hallway announced its arrival. Only a few patients were well enough to join the staff in the subdued celebration.

How odd to start a new year in this place. With Jack Slade. Abby stared at his sleeping face. It wasn't a soft face, his life experiences had left their mark. He was only twenty-seven but his youth had been spent in harsh places.

Now he had some new bruises, a cut over his left eye. Luckily, it wasn't deep enough to need stitches and wouldn't leave a scar to mar his ruggedly handsome features.

However, some scars remained on the inside, hidden from view, but they were there. Jack probably had a collection of them. Of course, he'd never share them with Abby. They were little more than strangers really. She wondered why that knowledge should hurt.

No doubt he would be furious when he learned she'd claimed to be his wife. It was only temporary. Abby silenced an irrational pang of regret. Then, out of some deep well of emotion buried deep within, she reached over and gently kissed him. There was no response.

In fairy tales, all it took was one chaste kiss to turn a frog into a prince. With a sad whimsical smile, Abby acknowledged that fanciful transformation wasn't likely to happen in this case.

Nevertheless, she pressed her lips to his a second time and whispered, "Happy New Year, Jack."

Chapter Three

Jack woke in a small, dark hospital room. There was a window, but the blinds were closed. He had no idea if it was night or day. He squinted into the dim reaches of the room crammed with medical equipment. A machine monitored vital signs in little beeps and blips. Other sounds were muffled. How long had he been unconscious?

Hours?

Days?

His mouth felt thick and fuzzy. When he tried to move, he discovered his left arm was in a cast. His right hand was hooked up to an intravenous tube, dripping colorless fluids into a vein. His ribs hurt, but at least it no longer felt as if each breath would be his last.

He tried to lift his head, then groaned. It felt as if

an elephant was sitting on it! He remembered someone saying he had a mild concussion. It didn't feel
mild.

Okay, enough whining—he could deal with a head-
ache, and a few additional bumps and bruises. He'd
survived a lot worse. In fact, he was damn lucky to
be alive. Then, he remembered.

His leg!

His gaze flew to the bottom of the bed. Yes, his
left leg was there. Encased in a hip-to-toe white plaster cast, it was still attached at the hip. He'd only
dreamed it was gone. At the sight of it, he released a
harsh breath. They'd saved his leg.

So, Abby had kept her promise.

Imagine that.

Throughout the nightmarish experience, he'd felt
her presence every step of the way. He should be
grateful for her help—and he was—but that was it.
He'd be a fool to care about *Miss Abigail*. There, he'd
put her in her rightful place—far above him—a firm
reminder that she was way out of his league.

That decided, he looked around the empty room.

So, where the hell was she now?

Jack turned expectantly at the sound of the door
opening, but to his disappointment, it was only a
nurse.

Her rubber-soled shoes squished on the tiled floor
as she approached the bed. He read the name on her
tag—she didn't look like a Tammy. More like Attila
the Hun.

"I see you're finally awake." She moved around

the bed as she checked various gauges on the equipment. "Anesthesia affects some people that way."

Jack got dizzy trying to follow her. Wishing she'd stand still, he ran his tongue over his lips, then tried to find his voice. "How long have I been here?"

"You were admitted three days ago." While he digested that piece of information, she added, "Does anything hurt?"

Everything hurt, but that wasn't the worst of it.

"I can't feel my leg," he said, rawly stating his deepest fear. He could plainly see it. He just couldn't feel it!

Tammy gave him a long sympathetic look. "The tests show the spinal column is intact, but there's some bruising and swelling."

Okay, that explained it, he supposed. His spine had been crushed—he remembered someone mentioning that. "So, how long before I get some feeling back?"

While he waited for a straight answer, she busily fluffed up his pillow, tucked in a sheet. "These things take time."

Things?

What things? They were talking about his leg. He couldn't go through life without it.

She asked, "Is there anything else?"

Apparently, he wasn't going to get any more information out of her. So, he settled for something more immediate. "I could use some water. My mouth feels as if I swallowed a bucket of sand."

"I'll get some ice chips. Your wife should be right back. She'll be so pleased to see you're awake."

His wife?

That caught his undivided attention.

"My what?" Jack's voice betrayed his amazement.

When, how and where—not to mention why—had he acquired a wife? He didn't get another word out before the nurse stuck a plastic thermometer in his mouth.

"Abby's a lovely girl."

"Mmm," Jack mouthed around the thermometer in agreement. He couldn't argue as a mental image of Abigail Pierce invaded his thoughts. Tall and slender, she was calm and reserved, naturally elegant with her long dark hair and pale skin.

There was a polished refinement about her that screamed *don't touch me.* It wasn't packaged or faked. And every time Jack saw her, he wanted to mess up that perfection, shatter the image, take her hair down. And touch her.

As if on cue, Abigail arrived.

She stopped in the doorway, her eyes widening at the sight of him. Her hazel eyes were rimmed in gold and reflected every mood. "Jack!" She looked shocked.

For crying out loud, who had she expected to find?

Jack mumbled something around the thermometer.

"Good morning," Abby said. It wasn't exactly original, but he was tempted to smile because when he was trapped on that mountain, he'd wondered if he'd ever see the dawn of another day. But this was no time to get all sentimental.

He needed some answers from *his wife.*

His brow creased at the reminder.

Normally confident, Abby looked tense as she

glanced from Jack to the nurse, then back again. "It's good to see you awake. You look better."

Finally, the nurse removed the thermometer from Jack's mouth. He grinned—or tried to. "Liar."

Abigail blushed, which intrigued him. For a brunette, she had very fair skin. Her hair was a rich deep shade of brown with highlights that gleamed red in the sun. She wore it held back with a silver clasp. Her clothes were tailored. Nothing fussy or overly feminine, but on her it looked good.

Before he got carried away with admiration, he could see pity in her eyes and refused to betray any sign of weakness. In any case, he had a lot of things to say to her.

Under the nurse's watchful eye, Abby brushed a fleeting kiss against his mouth.

That shocked Jack into an automatic response. He kissed her back. There was no pressure, the light contact lasted a fraction of a second, but it left an indelible impression of sweetness he hadn't expected. She looked startled when she pulled back.

Abigail Pierce always seemed so cool, almost frigid, with that reserved air. So, what the hell was going on? She'd kissed him. So what? Jack knew she wouldn't be half as brave if he wasn't all tied up—literally—with one arm in a cast, and another hooked up to an intravenous.

Obviously a romantic, Tammy said, "Your wife arranged to fly a specialist up from Boston in the middle of the night. And on New Year's Eve to boot. She sure was determined." The nurse spoke in obvious awe.

"I'll bet." Jack's sarcasm earned him a withering look from Abigail. With the Pierce family connections, she could get anyone to do her bidding, which only served to point out their insurmountable differences.

Tammy smiled. "Well, I'll leave you two lovebirds alone. Only short visits are allowed. You both could use some rest. Your wife hasn't left your side in days."

There it was again.

His wife.

And Abigail hadn't denied it.

After Tammy left, the two lovebirds glared at each other. Jack supposed he should be grateful. But he wasn't. He felt trapped. Once, wrongly accused, he'd gone to prison and served time for a crime he didn't commit. He felt that way now.

The memory of that harsh time was in his voice when he said, "All right, Abigail, let's get this over with. What's going on here?"

She looked extremely uncomfortable. "I know this must seem confusing. Please don't be angry."

"Can you blame me!" he snapped, feeling as if he stood on a precipice. He put every ounce of skepticism into the words, "Clue me in. What's the wifely act all about?"

"There is a logical explanation."

"Then, let's have it."

She slipped her hands into her pockets. Despite the casual pose, Jack wasn't fooled for a minute. She cleared her throat. "I don't know how much you recall about the airlift. You were so terribly hurt, and someone had to go with you.''

''Why?''

Her eyes widened. ''Well, because you couldn't go alone. And since only immediate family are permitted on board the rescue helicopter, I told them I was your wife.'' She ignored his muttered expletive. ''It was the only way. When we got to the hospital, the situation simply got out of control.''

Jack didn't get it. Either his thinking was fuzzy, or Abby wasn't making much sense. He needed to be absolutely clear on this. ''So, you told them we were married?''

She took a breath. ''Once we got here, I never actually said anything, everyone just assumed we were married.''

''And you let them believe a lie?''

She sighed. ''Well, yes.''

He lifted his brow in amazement. ''That's it?''

''Mmm,'' she murmured to his added frustration. ''I did sign the admission form.''

''You put it in writing.'' Jack took a much-needed breath. The movement hurt his ribs, but he didn't reveal his discomfort. Getting to the bottom of this was more important than a few broken bones. Those would heal in time. But the emotions he was feeling wouldn't go away in a hurry. What was he feeling? Confusion? What game was she playing at? ''How did you manage to fool the entire hospital staff?''

She stiffened. ''No one asked questions. I really didn't have any choice. The doctor was going to operate. He refused to rule out an amputation. I let him assume I was your wife. He finally agreed to wait until an orthopedic specialist could fly up from Boston. You asked me to save your leg. And I did. The only way I knew."

"By claiming we're married?" he snapped in disbelief.

"Exactly. There was no other way," she said heatedly. "You don't think I'd go through all this for any other reason?"

His eyes narrowed. "Why would I think that? You've got Seth Powers back home on a short leash. The guy's obviously nuts about you."

"He doesn't own me."

"He acts as if he does. He's going to be furious when he hears about this."

"I don't see why he has to know. After all, I did what I thought necessary, now it's over. And even if Seth should find out, I'm sure he'll understand when I explain the circumstances."

Jack wondered about that—if she belonged to *him,* he wouldn't be that understanding. "Then he's a fool."

"Because he trusts me?"

"You said it, I didn't."

Abby sighed. "This isn't getting us anywhere."

Abby didn't know what else to say.

Of course, there was no logical explanation for what she'd done. She must have lost her mind. How could she have claimed this man, even temporarily? Being in the same room with him was like entering a cage with a live tiger. Even in Jack's weakened condition, he was still a major threat. His blue eyes, so often remote and indifferent, burned into hers, scouring her with a look that made her heart beat faster with alarm—and something more threatening.

His face was gray, and his mouth tight with pain— it was there in his eyes. How could it hurt so much to see him hurting?

His weariness apparent, he leaned back against the pillows and said dryly, "Did you ever think that maybe I'm not worth it? Maybe you should have left me on that mountainside."

She gasped at the words. "Don't say that! Don't even think such a thing. I've gone to all this trouble, don't you dare let me down now!"

"All right." He laughed, obviously surprised at her vehement response, then gently mocked her with the words, "You may still live to regret it."

Was that a promise or a threat?

They stared at each other, confused and conflicted.

Abby broke the awkward silence. "In any case, the situation is only temporary until I go home."

"Right."

His easy agreement hurt, which made absolutely no sense at all! "Until then, telling the hospital would only prove awkward for everyone concerned." Of course, she had no logical explanation for what she'd done. "We could keep up the pretense for now."

He taunted her. "And how do you suggest we accomplish that?"

"You could start by calling me Abby."

"That should do it for the staff. If the news doesn't leak any further, we should be able to keep a lid on it."

"I hope so."

He let out an exasperated breath. "If this gets back to Henderson, I'll never live it down."

Abby stifled a laugh. He was worried about what *his* friends would say. What about her friends? Her family? Her mother didn't even approve of Seth. What on earth would she say about Jack? With luck, her mother would never have to know.

"Well, I'm not planning on telling anyone," she assured him. "In the meantime, is there anything you need?"

He nodded. "Some ice chips."

"What?" The simple request startled her.

"The nurse said she'd bring some ice chips, she must have forgotten." He looked pale, his patience with their situation obviously worn thin.

With her own nerves on edge, Abby grasped the excuse and left. She found an ice machine in the staff kitchen, and filled a paper cup with ice chips.

That didn't take very long.

His eyes were closed when she returned to his room. Assuming he must be asleep, she set the cup down on the rolling bedside table, edging it closer. She was startled when he opened his eyes and murmured, "Thanks."

"I promised the nurse I wouldn't tire you. I should go," she said, her emotions brittle, aware that she was looking for an escape from all the tension. Their relationship had always been strained. Now, it was almost to the breaking point. "I'll just leave the ice."

His eyes flickered over her. "Sure."

Stung by his indifference, she rushed into explanations, more excuses. "I should check into a hotel. I'll come by later, just to see if you're okay."

His mouth twisted with a mocking, "Don't go to any trouble on my account."

"No trouble."

That was an understatement.

After the door closed behind her, Jack's grin faded.

Blocking everything out, he stared at the white ceiling. A light hung in the middle, casting a pale round yellowish glow. If he focused on that, he wouldn't feel the waves of pain. He could ask for more painkillers, but he knew what those could do. He had enough problems without adding an addiction to the list.

He'd been in a lot of fixes, there had to be some way out of this one. His gaze fell to his injured leg. He stared at his foot, willing it to move. Nothing happened.

What weren't the doctors telling him?

There was swelling around the spinal cord. What if it wasn't that simple? Wearily, he closed his eyes.

Pain clawed at him, but his leg remained curiously numb. He tried to put it all out of his mind, focusing on something else. That something was Abigail…Abby.

She was playing some sort of game, pretending to be his wife. What were the advantages, the risks? They were totally mismatched, and he didn't know the rules.

An image of her appeared…Abby clearly flustered when she'd kissed him. Forced to pretend she actually enjoyed it, she'd looked so annoyed, like a treed cat, spitting and clawing, unable to scratch his eyes out when he'd kissed her back in the nurse's presence.

He smiled.

Much better.

Abby desperately needed a break. She hadn't left the hospital in days. Although everyone was kind and helpful, they expected her to behave like a wife. *Jack's wife.* Letting him in on their secret had been difficult. At the moment, continuing the pretence was beyond her acting ability.

On her way out of the hospital, Abby caught a fleeting glimpse of Jack's surgeon. Determined to question the doctor about Jack's prognosis, she followed him down one hall, then another. She caught up with him near an exit.

"Excuse me, I wonder if I could have a moment, I'd like to discuss a patient—Jack Slade."

The doctor was surprisingly youthful considering his reputation as a first-rate orthopedic surgeon. Obviously in a hurry, he glanced at his watch. "I have a plane to catch."

"This won't take long." Abby needed to tie up a few loose ends before going home to Henderson. She might not be Jack's wife, but she was the only available person who could run interference with the hospital staff and speak on his behalf. "I can't thank you enough for everything you've done."

"Don't thank me just yet," he said bluntly.

Swallowing hard, Abby braced herself for more bad news. "But I was told the surgery went well."

"Your husband will recover. Technically, we saved his leg. As you know, the surgery is experimental and there's no guarantee how much use the leg will be to him."

Abby absorbed the shock. "So what *can* be done for him? I don't care what it costs."

"It's not a matter of cost," he said more gently.

"I'm sorry, I didn't mean—"

"There are things that can be done. Maintaining his general physical and mental health are vital. When it's time, he'll be transferred to a rehabilitation unit. And that's where the tough part comes in. That's where you come in."

She bit her lip. "I don't understand."

"Over the next months, he's going to be fighting an uphill battle. Much of his success will depend on his desire to get well. He's going to need you."

Months!

Reminded that she was playing a temporary role, Abby saw all the pitfalls she'd ignored before. How could she have thought to escape the repercussions of pretending to be Jack's wife?

"Yes, of course," she agreed, but wasn't this taking pretence too far?

"This must seem overwhelming. It's all going to take time. I hope he's the patient sort."

Abby smiled. "No, he's not." Jack burned energy just standing still, which made his injuries all the more tragic.

The doctor glanced at his wristwatch again. "I still have a plane to catch."

"But what do I tell Jack?"

"The truth—when you think he's ready to hear it."

"When will that be?"

He left her with an ambiguous, "You'll know."

How would she know?

Jack was a virtual stranger. They'd rarely spoken before his accident. Once, Jack had driven her home and they'd hardly exchanged a word. She'd given him directions to her house. He'd acted as if he couldn't wait to get rid of her. The feeling had been entirely mutual. Abby had never spent a more uncomfortable fifteen minutes. Until now.

She had no idea what constituted Jack's inner thoughts or feelings—if he had any.

Abby walked down a corridor, then another. Like a maze, every hallway looked alike, every door remained closed. She saw an open door. She walked hastily toward it, anxious to find a way out. But instead of an exit, she found herself in a large room with a wall of sunlit windows overlooking park-like grounds and a pond. There was no way out.

Startled, she stared at her own reflection in the glass. Her face was drawn, her eyes looked bruised from lack of sleep. Yes, she'd lost sleep over Jack Slade. She was in grave danger of losing much, much more. Like a diamond in the rough, Jack had a devastating charm she couldn't deny.

Despite that undeniable threat, she didn't regret her decision to pose as his wife, thereby insisting his surgery be delayed until a specialist could be consulted. The hospital staff had never questioned her claim. If the facts were to come out now, there might be legal repercussions. At the very least, the situation would be embarrassing for everyone concerned.

She smiled faintly, recalling her mother's frequent warning that pride would be Abby's downfall. She really had no choice but to continue the deception. Earlier, she'd been relieved when Jack had agreed. It was too late for second thoughts now.

So, why was she having them?

She was so mixed up. She'd once heard that if you saved a life, that person belonged to you. Abby shuddered at the thought.

Moments later, she found an exit and pushed her way through a set of heavy revolving doors. She stood on the pavement, breathing in the frigid air. The wind carried a bite. Wrapping her coat around her, she began to walk. She passed some skaters on the frozen pond. It all seemed so normal, yet nothing in her life felt real.

She checked into a nearby hotel.

The desk clerk raised an eyebrow at her lack of luggage. "How long do you plan to stay?"

"A day or two." Abby had no idea. In all conscience, could she go back to Henderson and leave Jack to cope on his own? She couldn't think of that now.

Her hotel room wasn't luxurious, but it was more than adequate. After a long soak in the bathtub, she wrapped herself in a terry bathrobe provided by the hotel.

With distaste, she gazed at the clothes she'd worn for the past three days. Her lack of wardrobe wasn't insurmountable. A phone call to a department store soon resolved the problem. A salesclerk promised to have a selection of lingerie and casual outfits in Abby's size sent to the hotel for approval. That dealt with, Abby hung up.

After living in a small town for the last three months, she'd almost forgotten the conveniences of city living—not that she had missed it. She'd moved back to help Drew reopen the sawmill. Her family had closed it down and moved away several years ago, and Abby had gone with them. Returning to Henderson had created some unnecessary complications to her life. For one thing, Seth Powers had read more into her decision than she'd intended. She'd once had a crush on him but that was a long time ago.

Her parents disapproved of Seth, a small-town sheriff. They wanted Abby to marry well—meaning upward. What would they think of Jack?

Abby felt weak at the mere thought.

Or maybe she was weak with hunger?

Reminded that she hadn't eaten a decent meal in days, Abby ordered room service. "A mushroom omelet, toast and raspberry tea, if you have it."

While waiting for the meal, she picked up the phone and dialed her brother's phone number. "Hi, Drew. It's me."

His voice sounded warm and familiar. "I wondered when you'd get around to calling. How's Jack?"

"I'm worried about him," she said after a moment's hesitation. "The doctor's aren't promising anything much."

"Does Jack know?"

"Not yet." On impulse, she added, "If I decide to stay for a while, do you think someone could fill in for me at the sawmill? The situation here is complicated."

"Tell me about it," he said dryly. "It's all over the newspapers. A reporter dug up Jack's prison record. He's not going to be happy about that."

Abby gasped. "So everyone knows?"

"You're off the hook. Everyone here knows better than to believe everything they read. They assumed the reporter messed up the part about you and Jack being married."

"Well, that's one less thing to worry about."

"That doesn't clear everything up. Do you know what you're doing?"

She laughed, admitting shakily, "No."

Drew didn't sound amused. "Abby, I'm not going to tell you what to do with your life. I care about you. Jack is my friend, so is Seth. Someone's bound to get hurt."

"Seth will understand." He always did.

"Well, you'd better get your story straight because he's on his way. He intends to bring you back with him." Drew changed the subject. "By the way, Olivia sends her love. You missed our New Year's announcement—we're having a baby."

Abby could hear the emotion in his voice. Drew's good news emphasized the emptiness in her own life. "That's wonderful. I'm so happy for you both."

"Yes, it's pretty great."

The conversation ended on that lighter note.

After hanging up, Abby dialed room service and

ordered a newspaper. Fifteen minutes later, a hotel steward delivered her meal with a newspaper folded on the tray. After tipping him generously, Abby ignored the food and reached for the paper.

Splashed across the front page, the eye-catching headline said it all—Dramatic Air Rescue.

The reporter had romanticized the event—a devoted young wife going to her husband's rescue. They were identified simply as Jack and Abby Slade.

Abby sighed.

So much for keeping a lid on it!

Chapter Four

In smaller print, the subtitle—Ex-con Injured in Logging Accident—had more impact. The reporter had gone to great lengths to dig up old news.

There was quite a lot. Feeling like an intruder invading Jack's private life, Abby skimmed over the details. At the age of twenty, he'd served three years in prison for a crime he hadn't committed. Jack Slade was innocent. As if she needed convincing, Abby read that sentence twice.

Drew had tried to tell her that Jack was a victim of bad luck, but she'd refused to listen.

Was it easier to believe Jack was guilty?

Easier to dislike him?

Safer?

A knock at the door announced the arrival of the saleswoman from the department store. "I brought a selection of items for you to choose from. They're casual styles as you requested.'' She was carrying several boxes.

Abby opened the door wider. ''Just put them anywhere. How much do I owe you?''

''I wasn't sure about the colors. Wouldn't you like to look them over first?'' The woman handed her the bill.

Abby signed it, her family had an account at the store. ''I'm sure they'll be fine.'' She smiled politely to hide her impatience and saw the woman out.

According to her brother, Seth was on his way. Since he'd probably turn up at the hospital looking for her, she should be getting back. Under the circumstances, her wardrobe or lack of it was the last thing on her mind.

She normally wore tailored clothes, neutral colors, discreet makeup. What did it matter what she wore?

No one would notice.

Jack noticed.

In fact, he couldn't help but stare at Abby's altered appearance when she arrived. She hesitated a moment before she entered the hospital room, and suddenly, the sterile green room took on light. She removed her wool coat and set it aside. A bright jade-green sweater hugged her breasts; slim black slacks made her legs look longer, her hips round and womanly. Her face was flushed, her mouth was naturally pink, her eyes a shimmering hazel.

It took Jack a moment to realize she wasn't wearing makeup. Without it, she looked younger, more vulnerable, more accessible. He frowned. What was she up to now?

He couldn't fully trust her, Abby had too much money and too much time on her hands. She was a woman in search of a cause. And he was it. In all their dealings, he had to remember that. However, he hadn't always felt that way about Abby.

If fate didn't have a twisted sense of humor, he and Abby would never have crossed paths in a million years.

However, through mischance, he'd once shared a minimum-security prison cell with her brother. To say they'd hit it off would be a stretch. Until then, Drew had obviously played at life while Jack merely survived. Thus, better schooled in the art, Jack bailed Drew out of trouble with another inmate, and they became allies. A loner by choice, Jack had soon concluded that Drew had alienated everyone who once cared for him. The Pierce money hadn't cushioned his fall from grace and for the first time in his life, Drew was taking responsibility for his own mistakes. His parents had apparently disowned him. As far as Jack could tell, Abby was the only family member to stand by Drew.

Recalling the steady flow of letters she'd sent her brother in prison, Jack admired her loyalty. She'd written about college, her wacky roommates, her stern chemistry professor with the handlebar mustache. An average student, she'd loved art and music, hated math and chemistry, run a marathon and volunteered to work in a soup kitchen. One summer, she learned to water-ski, the next she worked at a camp for underprivileged children.

She'd sent pictures. To be honest, Jack had fallen just a little bit in love with Abby—the pretty girl with the pensive smile and soft mysterious eyes.

That was before he met Abigail.

The first day he'd applied for a job at the sawmill, she'd frozen him off with one look that should have put Jack exactly in his place—had he known where that was.

Now she spoke quietly, "The nurse said to notify her when you woke up," as if she didn't want to disturb him. It was too late for that—Jack's pulse had soared the moment she walked into the room.

"Go ahead. I'm not going anywhere." Apparently, neither was Abigail. He tried to shut out her voice, the soft floral scent of her perfume. "I wasn't expecting you."

After buzzing the nurse, Abby said, "Something came up."

"Let me guess—the newspaper article."

Her startled gaze shifted to the newspaper on the edge of the bedside stand. "I see you got a copy."

"The nurse brought it around." She'd also made the bed with him in it. By the time Tammy had completed the task, they were both exhausted. Between one thing and another, Jack was in a foul mood. "So, our little secret is out. We're married. You know, we could have avoided this mess by admitting the truth and clearing up the confusion at the start."

"I know." Abby twisted her hands together, stopping when his gaze followed the nervous gesture. She slid her hands into her pockets. "But I never thought it would get into the papers. It's too late to do anything about it now."

"We could explain the situation and get it over with."

"But that might create more headlines and involve the hospital in legalities. Besides, it would be awkward for everyone concerned." Meaning Abigail.

Jack smiled grimly. "And you don't think pretending to be married will be awkward?"

"It needn't be. This is a hospital," she pointed out in a reasonable tone that grated on his nerves. "No one asks personal questions unless it directly affects a patient's health. Please don't be angry."

"I'm not angry—I'm confused. Why did you do it?"

She shrugged. "Because you asked for my help. I know that sounds odd, but everything was happening so fast. I didn't have time to think. I just got carried along with the situation."

"What are your parents going to say?"

"They're away at the moment."

"That will buy you time, but nothing else."

Apparently, Abby had more pressing concerns. "Is everything the reporter wrote true?"

"More or less." Wrongly accused, he'd spent three years in prison before he was cleared of all charges. However, he'd left something behind in prison—his youth, his faith in the goodness of his fellow man. And his belief in tomorrow.

Abby frowned. "You never committed any crime.

When you first arrived in Henderson, why didn't you explain?''

"Because no one asked." Jack hoped she'd take the hint and change the subject. He'd spent time in prison—end of story. Almost. Eventually, he'd been set free—with apologies from the prosecutor, but nothing else. Well, *sorry* didn't win back your self-respect or hand you a job. Shackled by the bitter memory of a friend's betrayal, Jack was free of all emotional ties and determined to remain that way.

"You met my brother in prison. Drew made some mistakes, but he's made up for them. I'm very proud of him."

"He's a good man." Jack wondered where this conversation was going. As far as he could tell, Drew had turned his life around after his release. In quick order, he'd married, settled down and reopened the sawmill. With Olivia firmly in his corner, he was earning the respect of the townspeople who still doubted his sincerity. And his commitment. In some ways, the jury was still out when it came to Drew Pierce. He'd come a long way from the spoiled careless playboy in Jack's estimation. Prison could make or break a man. As Gran would say, "the same fire that melts butter forges steel." Jack frowned, wondering if the same could be said of him.

Abby continued. "He's worked hard to turn his life around."

Ah—so that was it. Jack smiled wearily. He'd arrived in Henderson with a chip on his shoulder and something to prove—to himself. Drew Pierce had owed him a favor and given him a job on a logging crew. Before the accident, things had been working out. That was then, this was now. Now, more than ever, Jack couldn't lower his guard and let people close—Abby topped the list. "You were afraid I'd drag him down again."

At the blunt accusation, she drew in a breath. "Something like that. Knowing you met Drew in jail, I—" Abby's voice drifted off. "I'm sorry." She seemed so genuine, appealing to him with a wide candid gaze. Didn't she know how vulnerable that made her? "I hope you can forgive me."

For once, Jack's cynicism failed him. If he wasn't more careful, he was going to begin to like Abigail Pierce! "Let's just drop it."

She persisted. "How did you and Drew become friends?"

"Do you really want the details?"

"Yes. I would."

Jack shrugged. "Drew rubbed some guys the wrong way. When they threatened to teach him a lesson, I made it clear they had to get through me first."

At the stark explanation, Abby shuddered. Forced to confront the harsh facts, she said, "How awful." In comparison, her life had been sheltered. She'd never risked anything, never failed, never reached any great heights.

Jack stared at her, his eyes challenging, the cool blue depths mocking her. "Too real for you?"

She swallowed hard. "It's difficult to imagine Drew in that sort of situation. And you were so young at the time. It wasn't right, you were innocent."

His mouth twisted in denial. "Look, don't go pinning any halos on me. I was no angel.'' From his expression, that was an understatement. ''But I didn't steal anything.''

''So, what happened?''

''A friend—someone I trusted—fixed me up with a job driving a truck interstate.'' This was obviously a sore subject; the words seemed dragged out of him. ''I was young and stupid, I never questioned where the stuff came from.''

''That's understandable.''

''A jury didn't think so. It turned out to be stolen tech equipment and I was caught with the goods.''

''But you were found innocent—eventually.''

''Yeah—I got out.''

''That's so unfair,'' she said.

''Life isn't always fair.''

''No, it isn't.'' Abby glanced away from the hard-won knowledge in his eyes. He'd opened up to her—it felt odd. Until this moment, they'd never had a coherent conversation.

Searching for a change of subject, Abby picked up the paper cup on the table. The ice had melted. With growing discomfort, she realized it had remained exactly where she'd left it on the bedside table earlier—out of Jack's reach. He couldn't use his hands. How he must hate that.

He'd never asked for help, and she'd never offered. Abby felt ashamed. Was she that self-absorbed? ''Why didn't you tell me you needed help?''

He shrugged. ''It's no big deal.''

According to him, it was a small thing—but it had huge implications. He was helpless. The knowledge settled over Abby's wary heart. Her conscience warred with a sense of self-preservation. No matter how she tried to avoid the truth, being tied to Jack meant more to her than a sham pretence. She couldn't just abandon him. Could she?

To her relief, the staff nurse arrived with a food tray. However, Abby's relief didn't last long.

"Mrs. Slade, we're all so pleased to see your husband doing so well."

Feeling her face redden under Jack's cynical smile, Abby nearly choked out the words, "Please, call me Abby."

"All right, Abby it is." The woman set the tray on a rolling bed table. "Jack needs help with this." She obviously expected Abby to take over with the feeding.

"I'm not sure I'll be any good at this."

The nurse smiled her encouragement. "It may feel awkward at first, but you'll do fine. Just see that he eats what's on the tray. He needs to regain his strength."

Once the nurse left, Abby lifted the lids off the food. "There's chicken broth." A rush of hot steam flushed her face. Or maybe it was Jack's intent frown. "Lime Jell-O."

"Lime?"

"And herbal tea." She added a straw and held it to his mouth. He sipped with obvious reluctance.

She'd never been this close to him. The cut over his eye hadn't required stitches. A white bandage covered it, the surrounding bruise was purplish. It looked painful. Unshaven, his beard was thick and black; he looked rough, and alarmingly worn-out after only a few sips of tea. When he coughed, his face went gray.

Abby wanted to do something—anything—to make his pain go away. But he would only resent her pity. Once he recovered his breath, she resumed feeding him.

After the tea, the chicken broth went down more easily.

"How about some Jell-O?" Before he could object, she aimed a spoonful at his mouth. That silenced him. Hmm. This could be interesting. Aware of his growing impatience, Abby continued to spoon-feed Jack.

With his eyes resenting her, he opened his mouth again, then swallowed. His voice was hoarse. "I've had enough."

Jack clamped his mouth shut.

He watched Abby's chin lift with that determined look he'd begun to recognize. As if by reflex, her mouth opened and she tempted him with, "Just one more."

Feeling like Adam taking a bite out of the apple, Jack accepted another spoonful of lime Jell-O. "That's it," he rasped on a harsher note than he'd intended.

Abby's hand shook. They both watched as a glob of Jell-O slid off the spoon then landed in the middle of his chest. "Oh, dear. Now look what you've done." She slid the tray to one side.

"That was your fault," he retorted, his irritation plain.

"You're a rotten patient," she said, attempting a

bit of humor, and failing badly. She was normally reserved, why couldn't she control her temper when it came to this man?

His eyes gleamed with the direct challenge. "That makes us even. You're no great shakes as a nurse."

"I'm trying."

At her surrender, he said gruffly, "You're doing okay."

As far as compliments went, it left a lot to be desired, but the words warmed Abby's heart. Was she so desperate for his approval?

Abby reached for a napkin and dabbed at his chest. To gain better access, she sat on the edge of his bed and leaned toward him. The hospital bed was alarmingly narrow. The Jell-O left a green stain on his white hospital gown.

She sighed. "I think that's the best I can do. But you've got some—just there." She swiped at the corner of his hard mouth. He groaned.

She lifted her gaze to his. "Am I hurting you?" Her eyes arrested when his blue eyes darkened, she ran a tongue over her suddenly dry lips. "Sorry."

"It's nothing." Man-like, he had to have the last word.

With a wry twist of his mouth, Jack hid his physical response from Abby. Inwardly, he cursed his bad luck. Here he was in the middle of his favorite male fantasy with Abigail Pierce sharing his bed and there wasn't a damn thing he could do about it! His hands were tied—literally.

She was so close. He stared at her bare pink mouth and felt her breath mingle with his. Her sweet delicate perfume vied with the sharp scent of antiseptic, the aura of illness.

Though wary, his gaze lifted to hers, catching the dazed confusion in her soft eyes.

Ah, so she felt it too.

The awareness.

It was raw and potent and undeniable. It was sweet and tempting. It was damned inconvenient—that's what it was.

Her eyes darkened. She shook her head—as if light-headed.

Jack felt a little light-headed himself.

Maybe it was the medication?

Maybe it was Abby?

He could feel her breasts against his chest as she bent closer. Was that her heart pounding erratically, or his? He'd never know the answer to that, or what *might* have happened between him and Abby if Seth Powers hadn't arrived in that dizzying moment of heightened awareness.

"Abby!" All it took was one word from Seth to separate them and send Abby into an obvious tailspin. "They told me I'd find you here."

"Seth." Flustered, she tugged her tunic-length sweater down over her hips—as if she had something to hide.

Jack had no idea how long the sheriff had been standing in the doorway watching them, but he suspected it was long enough for Seth to get the wrong idea.

The man's eyes were narrowed in obvious suspicion, but Seth was wrong. No matter how intimate

the situation might appear, Abby was in no immediate
danger of losing her heart—or anything else for that
matter—to Jack. She might feel pity but nothing
more. Jack had met girls like her before—do-gooders
who got their kicks out of reforming some poor jerk.
Well, it wasn't going to work on him.

Not that he needed reforming.

Seth greeted Jack with a laconic, "Looks like you
tangled with a skidder and lost."

"You should see the skidder," Jack said dryly,
earning him a clear glimmer of respect from Seth.

Despite the slight thaw, Jack had no use for law-
and-order types. He'd tangled with them once too often and had come out the loser. Prison had taught Jack
a lesson. Nothing in this life was worth the price of
his freedom. In Seth's world, everything was clear-
cut, black and white, while Jack's was gray without
definition or direction. And plenty of obstacles.

His manner openly possessive, Seth approached
Abby.

Deeply conscious of Jack's cynical gaze, Abby
averted her head, and Seth's kiss landed on her cheek.
She'd once thought her future was with Seth. But now
there was Jack. He made her feel awkward and unsure. And alive.

She felt flushed, unsure why Seth's quiet air of censure should make her feel so embarrassed.

Guilty.

Seth didn't own her.

No man did.

Abby wanted to scream it from the rooftops. But
with both men glaring at each other—then at her—

she decided it was time to put an end to this encounter. "Seth, I think we should go. Jack must be tired. Oh, I forgot—the ice chips."

"Forget it. Tammy will be around," Jack said, making no attempt to hide his relief at their leaving.

Abby frowned. "Tammy?"

"My nurse." The words were dry.

"Yes, of course."

Jack smiled crookedly. Abby had no idea what that smug smile meant. Did he think she was jealous? She hadn't failed to notice how the nurses flocked around him. Some were young and attractive.

Jack had the last word. "Have a nice evening."

That was that. She was free to go. So why did she feel as if an anchor was weighing her down, why did she feel as if she wanted to argue? Why did she feel as if she wanted to see exactly what this Tammy looked like?

How in the world had her life become so complicated? Only short days ago, she'd been contemplating a possible future with Seth. Now she wasn't sure how she felt. If she was in love with Seth, wouldn't she know? She was drawn to Jack. Physically attracted. He frightened her with the depths of his need—both emotional and physical. Should love be all-consuming, a flash-fire of desire? Or a steady flame to keep her warm when the flames of infatuation burned low?

Out of all the confusion, one thing was clear—she didn't know her own mind.

Or heart.

Abby gathered her coat while Jack and Seth exchanged a few words, both obviously relieved to get past the polite niceties. They were opposites in both looks and temperament. One dark, one fair. Seth was patient, Jack was not. Seth was comfortable and safe, Jack was the unknown. Seth was in a hurry to leave, Jack wasn't going anywhere at the moment.

"See you later," Seth said in parting.

He took Abby's hand, they walked down the hall, past the nurses' station. Abby glanced at the man at her side. Seth stood inches taller than she. His hair was fair, his features strong and distinct with eyes that warmed when he looked at Abby and caught her staring.

"You look tired," he said. Even out of his official police uniform, his presence commanded respect. There was something so solid and respectable about him. So comforting.

Why couldn't life be simple?

Abby had yet to come to terms with her own identity. The simple truth was that she wanted to experience life with all its highs and lows.

Why couldn't she love Seth?

Abby was tempted to lean on him, but didn't. "I checked into a hotel this afternoon, but I couldn't seem to relax."

"I'll get a room. We can have an early dinner. I'd like to get an early start home in the morning."

Seth was being considerate, assuming she would fall in with his plans. And normally, she would have, but this time, Abby resisted. "Actually, I planned to stay here a couple of extra days, just to make sure Jack's all right."

Seth smiled tightly, but he didn't argue. "I can wait."

Abby sighed.

Add patience to Seth's long list of virtues.

He'd already waited six years for her.

Chapter Five

Hours later, Jack was relieved when the activity in the intensive care unit died down. All was silent—except for the dripping faucet in the adjacent bathroom.

He tried to ignore it; he couldn't shut out the irritating sound. Like Chinese torture, it wore away at his patience until he was wide awake, staring at the ceiling. He lay trapped in his body, unable to get up and turn the damn thing off. He was helpless, dependent on others. The last time he'd trusted anyone, he'd landed in prison.

Drip, drip, drip.

Jack tried mind control, he tried counting backwards from a thousand to one. He was on five-hundred-and-sixty-three when he gave in to irritation. He stabbed the call bell attached to the bedrail.

A soothing disembodied voice came over an intercom above his head. "Can I help you? Do you need something to help you sleep?"

Not in the mood to be soothed or put to sleep by artificial means, Jack growled back, "The faucet's dripping. Just send someone to fix the damn thing!"

"I'll send someone right away."

Jack waited.

Patience.

He had it in short supply. From the looks of things, he was going to need a lot of it. Just when he was about to lose it again, a nurse arrived. To his surprise, it was Tammy, his day nurse.

"Everything okay in here?" she asked.

"The faucet's dripping," he snapped, hiding his relief at the sight of a familiar face.

Obviously accustomed to difficult patients, she smiled. "My, aren't we cranky." She turned off the faucet.

Blessed silence.

"Thanks," Jack said, somewhat mollified. "Don't they ever let you out of this place?"

"Someone called in sick, so I volunteered to work a double shift." She checked his vital signs, adjusted the tubes and wires linking him to various machines, then made a few notations on his chart. "Would you like something to help you sleep?"

"No, thanks." He appreciated her dealing unflinchingly with his physical limitations. There was no embarrassment, at least none on her part. "Why do you do this job?"

She batted her eyelashes at him. "Glamour. Excitement."

His chest hurt when he laughed. "Try again."

"Oh, I don't know, I've been doing this so long, I don't know how to do anything else. Besides, I love it. Why do you cut down trees?"

That was easy. "The freedom."

Tammy patted his shoulder. "You'll get it back, it takes time. How about some television?"

"Sure." He didn't bother to argue.

Tammy turned the set onto some late show before leaving. A comic was doing an old routine. Jack had seen it a dozen times before. He closed his eyes, the laugh track washed over him. He'd never felt so alone in his entire life.

At some point, he drifted into a light sleep—his chest felt crushed, he couldn't breathe. The sun was a red ball of fire in the sky. He felt hot—then cold. He shivered.

When would he feel warm again?

By morning, Jack's condition had worsened.

A nurse greeted Abby with the news. "His temperature's elevated. There's some lung congestion."

Abby glanced at Jack, who was sleeping. She was alarmed by the dark flush along his hard cheekbones, the shadows under his eyes. "But he was doing so much better."

The nurse tried to reassure her. "I know it seems like a setback, but it's not unusual in cases like this. The doctor ordered antibiotics, they should take effect before long. He pulled out his intravenous, I just restarted it. If you could keep him calm, that would be a big help. He's been restless. I think he misses you when you're not here.''

The words startled Abby. ''Yes, of course.'' It was the sort of thing anyone would say to a wife—but she wasn't Jack's wife.

''Let me know if you need anything,'' the nurse said before leaving.

Left alone with Jack, Abby pulled a chair close to the side of his bed. Apparently alerted by the movement, he murmured something.

Abby leaned closer to hear him say, ''Gran.'' He opened his eyes and looked squarely at her, his deepblue eyes glazed with fever. ''Don't go.''

With a sad smile, Abby wiped his brow with a damp cool cloth. ''I won't.'' She assumed he must be delirious.

Alert and fully conscious, Jack would never lower his guard and ask her to stay. Nevertheless, she remained at his side all day. By late evening, his temperature had soared.

When he shook with a violent chill, Abby drew a blanket over his chest, then wrapped it around his wide shoulders. He pushed her away, his arm thrashed about, straining at the intravenous tube.

Abby called for a nurse. ''Isn't there anything you can do?''

The nurse shook her head. ''If he pulls it out again, we may have to restrain him. Don't be alarmed. It's routine.''

Abby was getting so tired of that word. Perhaps it was business as usual for the hospital staff, but Jack's accident had sent his life—and Abby's—spinning out of control.

Once the nurse left, Abby tried giving him fluids. "Please, just a few sips."

He knocked the glass from her hand. His arm flailed about, threatening to dislodge his intravenous. The nurse had mentioned restraining Jack if it became necessary. Abby couldn't bear the thought. He nearly struck her with the heavy weight of his cast.

This time, Abby didn't call the nurse. She couldn't bear the thought of restraints, even if it was for his own protection. When he shuddered with another violent chill, she slipped off her shoes and climbed onto the narrow hospital bed. Aligning her body to fit against his side, she carefully placed her hand on his chest. He was so hurt, his body bruised and battered and broken, she was almost afraid to touch him.

Abby could feel his heart beating strongly against the palm of her hand. Aware that she would never have taken the liberty if he were awake, she wondered what it would be like to have a wife's right to touch him. Whatever emotions he evoked in her, her heart ached for him. Gradually, she felt him grow still, his breath stirred her hair. Abby had no intention of falling asleep, but she was exhausted.

During the long night, Jack felt cocooned in warmth. At one point, he opened his eyes and saw Abby, her long silky hair against his pillow, her face pressed against his shoulder. If he was dreaming or hallucinating, he hoped he never woke up.

In the morning, she was gone. Later, when she came in, Jack couldn't read her expression.

She spoke first. "It's good to see you awake. You slept through the last twenty-four hours."

His temperature had dropped to a low-grade fever. "I don't remember a thing." Jack watched her face lighten in relief. Though it nagged at him, he didn't want to ask the question that was uppermost on his mind—had Abby shared his bed and held him through the long night?

The possibility seemed too remote even to contemplate.

That evening, Abby's thoughts were filled with Jack. Unfortunately, she was having dinner with Seth. He wanted her to go home with him; she owed him some sort of answer.

Unable to shed her tension, she shared some of her worries, filling him in on the latest medical crisis. "The doctors suspect Jack's immune system might be rejecting the bone grafts. They checked, but the incision was clean."

Seth tried to change the subject. "Sounds like another hectic day. You must be tired."

"Jack was feeling better when I left."

Reaching for the menu, he smiled tightly. "Or you wouldn't be here—am I correct?"

"I didn't say that."

"Don't push it, Abby." Seth looked at his menu. "I'm in the mood for Italian, what looks good?"

Abby smiled. "Am I boring you?"

"Maybe I'm squeamish, but could we discuss bone grafts after dinner?"

Abby couldn't drop it. "The doctors aren't sure Jack will make a full recovery."

Seth set the menu aside. "All right, let's get this over with and talk about Jack Slade. I know, he's had a few tough breaks."

She lifted an eyebrow. "A few?"

"Okay—a lot of tough breaks, but he was a tough kid. He ran away from several foster homes, then hung out with a bad crowd long before he got into trouble. Don't let him con you into feeling sorry for him."

Abby sighed. "No one's ever given him a chance."

"And you're going to change all that? Repair his past? Rewrite his future?

"No," she said, drawing a breath. The restaurant was crowded, it was the wrong place to have this conversation. "That's not what I'm saying."

"You've done all you can. It's time to go home."

Abby shook her head. "Not yet. Even if all goes smoothly, Jack's recovery will take months. I can't leave until his prognosis is more definite."

Seth had ordered a rich red wine. The waiter came and filled their glasses. Abby lifted her glass and took a sip.

"This is very good," she murmured, hoping for a change of topic.

Seth stared at her in obvious frustration. "Are you still punishing me for investigating and arresting Drew five years ago? Let's be honest, is that what all this is about?"

"Of course not." She set her glass down, then folded her hands in her lap. However, she wasn't being completely honest. No matter how she tried to deny it, she'd never quite forgiven him for choosing duty over his professed love for her. Admittedly, she'd been an immature twenty-year old, and spoiled. "You were only doing your job."

"And you've never forgiven me."

"I was a child demanding blind devotion."

"I had a job to do. I made a choice," he said firmly.

The wrong choice.

The words remained unspoken between them.

Yes, Seth had hurt her. When Drew got into trouble, she'd foolishly asked Seth to choose between her and his duties as the sheriff. He'd chosen his job. Perhaps if he'd discussed his decision with her, she might have understood. However, he'd never taken her feelings into consideration. That was what hurt. Was it wrong to want more from a man?

Obviously unaware of her internal struggle, Seth said firmly, "I did what I had to do."

"I know." Abby knew Seth would always do the right thing—no matter what the cost. She apologized. "I'm sorry the subject came up."

All her life, Abby had watched her mother settle for less from a man who put personal ambition and pride above his family. Her father never had much interest in his only daughter. He'd pitted his sons against each other, then disowned Drew when he failed to live up to expectations. The price on her father's love was total obedience. Her mother was more soft-hearted, but she never questioned her husband's decisions, even when she didn't agree. That seemed so wrong to Abby. Was it wrong to want unconditional love?

Abby picked up the dinner menu. It had been a mistake to try and discuss Jack's condition with Seth. "How does the chicken cacciatore sound?"

Jack slept through an uneventful two days.

On the third day, a physical therapist assisted him with arm and leg movements, "to help with general circulation."

Jack chafed under the passive exercises. The therapist treated him with an off-hand kindness which he found oddly reassuring. Apparently she wasn't too worried about his condition, so why should he be? His progress was slow, impeded by the casts on his arm and leg. For a man in a hurry, Jack's life was on hold.

After the therapist was done with him, his nurse helped him stand on his feet for what seemed like hours but was only five minutes. His head felt woozy when she helped him back to bed. All in all, he felt weak as a kitten.

Tammy patted his shoulder. "Don't worry, things will be easier next time."

He grinned cockily. "Who's worried?"

She didn't answer.

Now, he was worried.

With a sympathetic motherly cluck, Tammy gently tucked him back into bed, then left.

Enjoying a moment's solitude, Jack leaned back against the pillows in exhaustion. For a man recovering from major trauma, he wasn't getting much rest. The place was a zoo. Counting doctors, nurses, technicians, orderlies—and Abby—he'd had thirty-two visitors. The day wasn't half over—make that thirty-three. Seth Powers arrived.

Great.

"They told me I'd find Abby here." Seth looked around the small room suspiciously, as if he expected to find her lifeless body stashed away somewhere.

Jack said dryly, "She went down to the cafeteria for lunch. She'll be back."

Seth removed his hat, then took a seat, clearly prepared to wait for as long as it took. "I'm not in any hurry."

His gaze fell on Jack's cast. "Looks like they managed to patch you up. How's it going?"

For some reason, Jack didn't particularly like Seth Powers, but he could play the game. "I'm surviving."

Apparently the animosity was mutual. A hard note crept into Seth's voice. "The staff seems to think you two are actually married."

Jack shrugged. "Things got mixed up in admissions. The newspapers picked up the story. At that point, explanations would have proved awkward. Abby didn't want to create an embarrassing situation, so we agreed to let things stand."

"You agreed?"

"Why not?" Jack hoped Seth would swallow the explanation because it didn't make a lick of sense, even to him. "Anyway, does it matter what the staff thinks? We know what's real and what isn't."

"Just remember that one small detail. And here's something else. Don't try anything with Abby."

Jack smiled coolly. Seth had nothing to worry about. But why make it easy on the guy? In any contest, Jack knew who the loser would be. In terms of a future, he had nothing to offer a woman like Abby. He'd be a fool to consider competing with Seth for her affection—or anything else for that matter.

"In case you haven't noticed," Jack said, "I'm not in any condition to do anything."

Seth stood impatiently. "Right. Just see that you don't take advantage of Abby's soft heart."

A soft heart?

The last thing Jack wanted from Abby was pity. Besides, from what he'd observed, her heart was rock-solid and hardly at risk—at least not when it came to their fake relationship. The idea that she might fall for him under any circumstances was laughable. And intriguing.

Seth threw out a more direct challenge. "I came to take Abby home, back to Henderson."

Jack didn't argue.

He had nothing at stake here. Nevertheless, he tensed when Abby came back.

She walked into the room and saw Seth. She was visibly shaken and Jack was glad he hadn't taken the sheriff up on the challenge. When she flushed with obvious embarrassment, Jack figured he'd had a lucky escape.

"Seth," Abby greeted the fair-haired man. "I wasn't expecting you."

"I was at loose ends and decided to drop by," Seth replied. "Jack and I were just talking."

Her flush deepened. "I see."

Jack spoke up. "I never had a chance to thank Seth for organizing the rescue effort."

Seth frowned. "Don't thank me. Abby saved your life."

"What do you mean?"

"The night you turned up missing, Abby raised the alarm. When you didn't get back to the sawmill before closing time, she insisted Drew call out a search party." Seth added a few details. "If it weren't for her, you could have been out there all night. She saved your life."

Still skeptical, Jack glanced at Abby for confirmation.

She sighed. "When your truck wasn't in the parking lot, I informed Drew."

"I appreciate all the concern." Jack leaned back. So, he owed Abby a huge debt of gratitude, one he could never repay. The knowledge grated. He couldn't figure her out. What possible motive could she have in coming to his rescue? In his experience everyone had to have an angle. What was Abby's? "Even if it comes as a surprise," he added.

Seth said coolly, "Abby's full of surprises."

Jack didn't doubt that for a minute.

To his relief, Abby took charge of the situation. "I'm sorry if I kept you waiting, Seth."

"That's okay," Seth snapped, his patience apparently at an end. "I'm going home tomorrow."

From Abby's startled expression, Jack could only assume that was news to her.

Seth reached for her hand. "I'm hoping Abby will come with me, now that you're on the mend, Jack."

"Thanks." Jack wasn't sure how he felt about Abby leaving. Did he feel anything? Was that ache in his chest due to a cracked rib, or did he actually feel a sense of loss at the thought of Abby going off with the sheriff?

As usual, Seth was openly possessive, but Jack didn't sense the same response in Abby. In fact, he'd never seen any real sign of warmth in their relationship. Reminding himself that Abby's love life, or lack of it, was none of his business, Jack said, "Have a safe trip home."

Abby's smile was strained. "Take care of yourself."

"I will." He'd been doing that all his life. His eyes met hers, dismissing her concern. He didn't need anyone.

So, why did he feel so alone when she walked out?

After leaving Jack's room, Abby could hardly contain her temper. She was disappointed in Jack, annoyed with Seth.

Men!

"I don't recall deciding to go back to Henderson," she said in a tight voice when they entered an elevator.

Obviously unaware of her irritation, Seth punched the down button. "Look, you've done all you can. It's time to go home."

"How can you know that?" Even if all went well, Jack's recovery would take months, not days or weeks. How would he bear up under a long period of inactivity? How could she explain her unease to Seth when she couldn't understand herself? She settled for a simple, "Jack needs me."

"And I don't?"

At the accusation, Abby caught her breath. "I didn't say that." She wondered if Seth would ever forgive her for choosing Jack over him. "It's not the same."

Seth's mouth tightened. "That's too bad. But Jack Slade isn't really your concern."

"Isn't he?"

Seth leaned against the wall and stared at her, his eyes wounded, yet accusing.

Abby couldn't look away. Suddenly, she knew what she had to do. "Don't you understand? Jack needs me."

No matter how much her role chafed; and whether Jack Slade would ever admit it or not, he needed her. It was a heady feeling.

Seth dashed that notion with a few words. "I may be obtuse, but no, I don't understand. You don't owe Jack a damn thing. I'm asking you to come home with me."

Choices.

Ironically, Abby thought of ice melting in a paper cup. Jack was helpless, she couldn't let Seth's anger sway her. She had other priorities to consider.

"I have to stay," she said quietly, as the elevator carried them down, then came to a grinding stop.

"Why?"

Her decision made, she had to admit to an inner feeling of relief—which confused her. "Because Jack needs me." So simple. So complex. "And he has no one."

Seth smiled grimly. "He has you."

"That's not true." The words shocked her into a hasty denial. "You're mistaken."

He smiled grimly. "You don't even know, do you?"

"Know what?"

"You're in love with the guy."

Abby searched for words of denial. "You're wrong."

Seth raised a skeptical eyebrow. "Coming to his rescue wasn't enough. You've gone to the extreme of pretending to be his wife. Haven't you asked yourself why?" Shoulders set in anger, he walked off the elevator.

Abby rushed after him. "I wanted to help. That doesn't mean I have feelings for him." She laughed hollowly. "I'm not even sure I like him."

"Then prove it." He stopped so abruptly that Abby almost ran into his back. "Walk away from the situation. Right now. Before it's too late, before you get more tangled into his life and can't get out."

Abby held her ground. "What do you expect me to do?"

"You say Jack needs you." Seth took her hand and stared at it for a long moment before meeting her gaze squarely. "What do *you* need, Abby?"

What did she need?

"I don't know," she said, shocked into an admission, she wasn't proud of it. Had she spent her life trying to be a reflection of what others wanted from her—instead of the real thing?

Seth released her hand. "Then, maybe it's time you figured it out. I'm going home tomorrow morning. If you change your mind about coming with me, let me know.''

She said honestly, ''I don't know what to say.''

''Then, don't say anything right now. Sleep on it.''

This was reality. Faced with an ultimatum, she could deal with Seth's disappointment or walk away from Jack when he needed someone.

The easiest thing would be to walk away.

Then why did that seem so hard?

Chapter Six

It was barely daylight, but the hospital was already bustling. A nurse greeted Jack, "Good morning."

He mumbled something back. He was in a foul mood. He hadn't slept well. He wasn't sure why, but he knew it had absolutely nothing to do with the fact that Abby was on her way back to Henderson. Breakfast didn't help.

Tammy was assigned to him for the day. She fed him watered-down hot cereal that looked like wallpaper paste and tasted worse, only sweetened.

He looked at the metal teapot on the tray. The only item remotely familiar on the tray was orange juice.

After breakfast, he had a bedbath.

And a change of bed linens.

That exhausted him.

Time for a nap.

Around mid-morning, Tammy woke him up to give him a pill. She checked his lab reports, and made a few notes on his chart. She smiled her approval. "Fluid intake is good. We can get rid of the intravenous." She did so with amazing efficiency, then said, "How about sitting up in a chair?"

Once free, Jack flexed his hand. "Sounds good." Getting up in a chair was a major milestone.

Forget Abby. He was regaining control of his life.

That assumption was soon knocked back. It took a hydraulic lift and three people to get him out of bed. While a nurse guided him into a body sling, another protected his leg cast, and an aide picked up the slack—meaning various trailing tubes and paraphernalia.

"Altogether—one, two, three." They lifted. For a suspended moment, Jack felt weightless.

Abby arrived midway through the process.

Abby!

Jack barely had time to register her presence. By the time he landed in the chair he was cursing a blue streak. Under the best of circumstances, his hospital gown wasn't an ideal length for a man his height, six-foot-two. Held together by a couple of flimsy Velcro strips, the thing flapped open in the back and rode up in front. And from the evidence of Abby's blushes, Jack could only assume that cold draft he'd felt wasn't all his imagination.

With his face reddening at a faster rate than Abby's, Jack grabbed for a blanket and pulled it across his legs.

"Abby," he choked. He tried to shift his position in the chair, but remained oddly glued to one spot.

Her face flushed, nearly as shockingly pink as the silk shirt she was wearing, she bent and kissed him on the cheek, a fleeting touch of her lips. She cleared her throat.

"It's good to see you sitting up." Her voice trembled with restraint. He'd obviously shocked her.

A small laugh escaped her. She wore her hair down, long and silky and fine. She brushed it back off her shoulders.

Jack looked at her more closely. Lips sealed tight, she was holding her breath and trying very hard not to laugh at him. He supposed he must have appeared ludicrous.

He grinned. "Yeah, well, I try to be entertaining."

She laughed. "Well, you've certainly succeeded."

His smile stayed in place. "So, where's Seth?"

She sobered immediately. "He's gone back home."

"Good."

Abby waited for him to say more. It took her a few minutes to realize he wasn't going to add anything.

Stepping out of the way when the nurse brought extra pillows to arrange around Jack's leg for added support, Abby took a moment to recover. Jack had reduced her monumental decision to a few simple words. She smiled, vaguely amused. After all her soul-searching, she felt a calmness—a rightness.

She'd said good-bye to Seth that morning.

They hadn't parted on the best of terms, which saddened her. She'd chosen to stay with Jack, knowing

Seth would never forgive her. She had feelings for him, but it wasn't love, and it wasn't fair to keep pretending it could ever be anything else.

She didn't want to hurt Seth. She loved his family—his widowed mother and three sisters. But it wasn't enough. He deserved someone who loved him heart and soul.

Earlier, when she'd awkwardly tried to put these sentiments into words, he'd said, "Then it's over."

"Can't we still be friends?" It sounded trite, even to her.

Seth had said tightly, "Sure, fine—whatever you say."

And that was it.

There was no going back.

At one time, she'd hoped to rekindle all the sweet youthful feelings she'd once felt for Seth. He was safe and reliable, she'd known him most of her life. But it was an old dream. It was time to let go. She regretted hurting him and wished there had been some other way. After Seth left, she'd felt very alone.

But free.

A nurse was still fussing over Jack. She tucked a blanket around his shoulders. "We don't want you getting a chill."

"No, we don't," Jack said dryly. "Abby, have I introduced you to Tammy?"

So this was Tammy. Abby caught the gleam of amusement in his eyes. The woman looked old enough to be Jack's mother. "Thank you for taking such good care of Jack."

"My pleasure." Tammy smiled. "You make a lovely couple."

Abby flushed uncomfortably. "Thank you."

Once Jack was comfortable in the large vinyl chair, Tammy asked him, "Where do you want to sit—by the window or out in the hall?"

Jack reacted with a frown. He didn't know if he'd heard correctly. "Why would I want to be out in the hall?"

"For one thing, a change of scenery would be good for you. You haven't been out of this room in a week."

"I'm not up for public display." For some reason, he wasn't ready to leave the cocooned safety of this room, the mere thought of facing strangers in his condition put him in a cold sweat.

"The window it is," Tammy said. "Is he always this difficult?"

Abby sighed. "Always."

While Jack was recovering from that, Tammy rolled the chair over by the window where she left him.

The sun felt warm on his face.

His ribs ached. Hiding his discomfort from Abby, he eased into a more comfortable position. He was glad to see her, glad she'd decided to stay. However, there was one area that needed clarification.

"What about Seth?" he asked. "I thought you were going home with him." He deliberately kept his voice casual, his facial expression closed.

"I decided to stay in town for a while."

Jack lifted a skeptical eyebrow. "And Seth had nothing to say about it?"

"He wasn't pleased," she admitted in what was obviously an understatement.

"For what it's worth, I'm sorry."

Her eyes darkened. "This doesn't really have anything to do with you. Things weren't working out between Seth and me. It was time to end things before they got more complicated."

So, Abby didn't like complications. Was her neat little world so tidy, so free of loose ends? For a brief second, Jack almost felt sorry for Seth.

But then he shrugged that thought aside. "Okay, so now what?"

"I haven't been out of Henderson in months. While I'm here, I thought I'd catch up with a few old friends, maybe do some skiing. Do you like to ski?"

"No."

Her gaze flew to his leg cast. She flushed guiltily, then glanced away. "I'm sorry—that was insensitive of me."

"Abby, there's no need to apologize. You don't have to walk on eggshells. Maybe I'll try skiing when I'm better."

"Yes, of course," she agreed. "I could teach you. It would be fun. Downhill is exciting, but cross-country has its good points. In fact, it would probably be good therapy."

That would mean seeing more of Abby when he got out. "I'll keep that in mind." Continuing their relationship on a casual level might not be wise.

At his lack of enthusiasm, there was a small awkward pause.

Abby filled it, clearly determined to overlook his bad mood. "Anyway, while I'm here, I'd like to do some shopping, take in some end-of-season sales."

Jack breathed a sigh of relief. Of course, she wanted to shop. Why would he think she was staying out of some misplaced obligation to him?

"Oh, I almost forgot. I got you something." She produced a take-out bag which he hadn't noticed earlier. From it, she removed two foam cups. "I found this great little coffee shop nearby." She removed the lid and handed him a cup. "I ordered hazelnut with cream and sugar. Is that how you like it? I wasn't sure."

Jack was no longer sure of anything. It was amazing how little they knew about each other. Yet, there was this pull. Did Abby feel it as strongly as he did? Seth was gone. Jack wondered if they'd argued. But that was none of his business.

He intended to keep it that way.

"This is fine." He took a sip.

Abby stirred her coffee. "Tomorrow, I'll bring muffins."

Tomorrow.

Despite his acquired cynicism, Jack latched on to that one word. Another promise. Abby would be there to help him face another day. He wouldn't think beyond that. He didn't know what it meant, but it meant something.

Okay, so maybe he was glad he didn't have to face the unknown alone. She'd promised him tomorrow.

He wondered how many he could count on. At some point, Abby was bound to get bored—or give up on him.

In any case, he'd face that day when it came. For now, if she wanted to stick around, that was fine with him.

Later, while Jack rested, Abby retreated to the visitor's lounge. Coffee was available from a machine. She got a cup then looked around for an empty seat. Among the occupants, she recognized the yarn lady from the emergency room the first night Jack was admitted.

Abby felt a certain kinship. "We've never met but I've seen you around the hospital before."

The woman smiled vaguely. "Oh yes, I remember you." They exchanged introductions. "I'm Phyllis. I'm sure I read about you in the newspaper. Your husband was hurt in an awful accident, he has the leg injury."

"Yes." Although Abby didn't attempt to clarify her position in Jack's life, she felt guilty for not being completely honest. Living a lie—even a well-intentioned one—was far more difficult than she'd ever imagined.

"My son was hurt in a snowmobile accident. Theo's only seventeen, he has a head injury." Phyllis took a deep breath. "The doctors say he'll recover, they're optimistic."

"I'm sure he'll be fine." Feeling helpless, Abby had to look away. Her gaze fell on the yellow yarn. "That's a lovely color."

"It is, isn't it? Crocheting calms me. If you're going to be around here for any length of time, you'll need something to do. I'd be happy to teach you."

"I wouldn't know where to begin." Abby smiled politely but made no commitment. She had no intention of being around long enough to learn how to crochet.

Nevertheless, Abby was by Jack's side a week later when a team of doctors came by to check on his progress. They stood around his bed, prodding and poking Jack and murmuring words that only they could understand.

An intern said, "The femur's shattered, but the damage could have been a lot worse."

Jack grimaced but hung on to his temper. That was his femur they were discussing. Another intern who didn't look old enough to shave glanced over the X-rays. "You're right. Just missed the patella by a hair."

Finally, Jack's patience snapped. "What is a patella and where the hell is it?"

The intern looked at him in surprise. "It's the knee-cap."

"Oh."

Feeling Jack's tension, Abby placed a hand on his shoulder. "I'm afraid I don't understand either. Could you explain?"

Secretly, she was pleased at Jack's show of emotion. Until now, he'd been entirely too passive. Any change, even anger, was a positive sign, an important step in the healing process. Jack was beginning to fight back.

The intern took out a pad of paper and sketched a quick anatomy lesson for Jack, throwing in a few technical terms.

Jack got lost between the tibia and the fibula. Now, he was sorry he'd asked. "Okay, I get it," he said, putting an end to it.

The doctor checked his injured leg. "Can you feel that?"

Jack shook his head. "Am I supposed to?"

"How about that?"

"No."

To Jack's frustration, the doctor frowned. "Don't worry about it. It's early days. Someone will talk to you about a wheelchair. You might want to think about customizing one."

"Is that necessary?"

"With physical therapy, you'll graduate from crutches and a walker to a cane. But you'll need a wheelchair as backup for some time."

Jack drew in a shallow breath. He didn't want to think that far ahead. "What's next?"

"As soon as there's an opening, you'll be transferred to a rehabilitation unit. That will start the process of getting you ready to go home."

There was only one thing Jack wanted to know, "How long will all this take?" For a man in a hurry, his life was on hold.

"That all depends on you."

The ball was in Jack's court.

After the team of doctors left, Jack tried to absorb

all they'd said—which wasn't much. In fact, he was more worried about what they hadn't told him. However, one thing was clear. His recovery was going to be a long, slow process.

He laughed harshly. "Sounds as if I need to get used to this place."

"Jack," Abby said softly. She took his hand, pressing it between both of her own. "Time will pass more quickly than you think." She took a deep breath. "You'll get better, I know you will. Just don't give up."

For a long moment, Jack said nothing. He looked down at their linked hands. He was tempted to cling, instead he pulled his hand free. She didn't try to hang on.

"I don't have any other choice." Hiding his doubts, Jack turned away from the sympathy in her eyes. He looked out at the snow-capped pine trees. The sun had slipped behind a cloud. "I suppose we can postpone those skiing lessons."

When Abby left for the day, Jack's mood hit rock-bottom.

He'd rarely felt so down.

At length, he fell into an exhausted sleep.

Morning was still hours away when he woke, startled out of a drug-induced sleep, drenched in perspiration and filled with a gut-wrenching fear. Like a slow-motion replay, the edges of his dream began to recede—he was hanging on to the wheel of the skidder, rolling over and over, praying for his life.

He'd made it.

His gaze darted around the empty corners of the room. Was this the dream? Or reality? Gradually, he identified the shapes: the chair by the window, the bedside table.

Jack's pulse began to slow. In the daylight hours, he could hide his fears, but in the shadows of the night, his dreams haunted him. Since the accident, he'd existed in this no-man's-land where days and nights blended into one, nothing mattered but survival. At times, the pain in various parts of his body was intense, radiating in waves. It was better than no existence at all. Earlier, he'd asked his nurse to leave the window blinds open. From his position, he had a view of a wide expanse of sky.

Jack stared into that black void, and tried to make sense out of his situation. Horror, self-pity, anger and confusion vied with the fact that he should be grateful just to be alive. Against all odds, he'd survived. Surely, there had to be a reason. But what?

Jack tried to empty his mind of troubling thoughts. Still, they lingered. Why was this happening to him? What had he done, how could he have messed up so badly on the job?

Granted, he wasn't as experienced as the other loggers. As a result, he frequently got behind. On the day of the accident, despite the dimming daylight and his own fatigue, he'd made one more run. Just one more. It had turned out to be a fateful one when a deer appeared out of nowhere, squarely in the skidder's path.

Jack had responded on reflex, saving the deer instead of himself. And this was the result.

Why hadn't he gone home with the other men? Instead, he'd worked late, trying to prove himself, afraid to lose his job, afraid of having nothing.

Being nothing.

His life was a mess.

There was no one to blame but himself.

The story of his life.

A few days later, get-well cards began to arrive.

Abby sorted through a pile on his bedside table. "You've got mail from friends back home."

He considered them acquaintances.

Flipping through some, she read off the names of people from Henderson. "Here's one from Drew and Olivia."

Jack looked up curiously. "What do they have to say?"

Before opening the card, she said, "Did I mention they're having a baby?"

"No, you didn't. When?"

"Sometime in the summer." She opened the card, smiling as she told him, "They send their love. They can't come because Olivia is suffering from morning sickness."

Jack smiled. "So Drew's going to be a father."

Hard to imagine his former cell-mate married and settled down, expecting a baby. Drew's life had changed for the better when he'd found Olivia. Apparently all it took was the right woman. That had worked for Drew, but Jack had no intention of learning to depend on anyone. That was for fools.

Abby opened the window shades. "It's a beautiful day."

She was the one bright spot. A wool sweater the color of spring daffodils softened her appearance. She wore pale lipstick, the blush looked natural. She looked so touchable. The sun was shining brightly around her, finding the reddish highlights in her hair. Sun and shadow played over her breasts and narrow waist, so feminine and delicate.

She leaned her hip against the windowsill. There was that intriguing wariness before she spoke, as if he made her uncomfortable. The feeling was mutual.

Considering all their differences, Jack wasn't surprised when she clearly had to search for a neutral topic of conversation. "It snowed last night—just a couple of inches."

Enjoying the view of Abby from his bed, Jack leaned back, prepared to discuss the weather for as long as she wanted. "Is it cold outside?"

"It's above freezing."

The temperature wasn't much warmer inside.

Chapter Seven

When Jack's mood didn't improve over the next few days, Abby decided he needed a distraction. She brought him a plant, a prickly cactus, which she set on a windowsill where it would get maximum exposure to the winter sunlight.

His mouth twitched. "Is that a hint?"

Abby confessed, "I thought it might cheer you up. Now that you're sitting up every day, I thought you could use a couple of additions to your wardrobe."

She'd purchased a bathrobe, slippers, pajamas. The wool robe was deep burgundy. And the slippers were a soft tan suede lined in warm wool pile. He only needed one slipper.

"I guessed at the size." She slid it onto his right foot. "It fits." His bare toes stuck out of the cast on his left foot.

Abby felt a sharp pang in the region of her heart at that sign of his vulnerability. Why did a man's bare foot seem so—so naked? Averting her face so he wouldn't read her troubled expression, she bundled up the empty boxes and bags.

"Thanks," he said, clearly not accustomed to accepting gifts from anyone. "You didn't have to get all this."

"I wanted to," Abby insisted, refusing to let his attitude dim her pleasure in giving. "Is there anything else you need?"

He frowned for a long moment before coming up with something. "I had a watch when I came in here. I haven't seen any sign of it—or my wallet."

"I'm sorry. When you were admitted, a nurse gave me a valuables envelope." Abby dug a thick brown envelope out of her coat pocket, then handed it to him. "I forgot all about it."

Jack drew out the items—a worn brown leather wallet, a digital watch, a compass and a chain with a St. Christopher medal—he'd once been a truck driver, a travelling man. There was also a ring threaded on the chain.

Weighing it in his hand, he seemed to hesitate again before removing it, then reaching for Abby's left hand and sliding the ring on the third finger before she could raise an objection.

"As long as we're going to pretend to be married, we might as well get this part right. The ring belonged to my grandmother," he said on a husky note. "She was the only family I had."

Through a veil of unshed tears, Abby stared at the

small perfect diamond set into a thin gold band. "I can't possibly wear this." She tried to remove it, but it stuck.

He frowned. "Why not? I know it isn't much, but—"

"It isn't that," she interrupted, dismayed that he'd misunderstood her so completely. "This ring obviously belonged to someone very precious in your life. Your grandmother loved you." Abby had no intention of letting herself love Jack. The risk of getting hurt was too great, almost guaranteed. "You should save it for someone you love, someone special who means as much to you as this ring does."

Jack refused to take it back. "You saved my life. In my book, that makes you special." He smiled warily. "Don't take that to mean anything personal."

Their gazes met, locked.

"I won't." Feeling a little light-headed when he smiled at her, Abby wondered how she could remain emotionally detached for the duration of this pretend marriage—however brief it might turn out to be. It had already dragged out longer than first intended.

Each looked away. The moment felt awkward, as if they'd peeled back one too many layers.

Jack stared at the plant on the windowsill, then laughed. "No one's ever given me a plant before. I don't have the vaguest idea how to take care of it."

"It comes with instructions." If only everything in life were that easy to arrange, Abby thought, recalling how risky and complicated her life had become since she'd attached herself to this wounded man. "It's guaranteed to blossom."

The cactus sat on the windowsill in a halo of light. Jack couldn't ignore it.

The mottled green plant had spikes that prevented anyone from getting too close. Supposedly, a cactus could bloom in a desert without a drop of water. But he had his doubts about this squat little plant. So, she'd brought him a plant. An ugly plant.

So what?

Jack shifted his gaze away from the prickly cactus—and Abby. For crying out loud, he wasn't about to get all weak and sentimental over a plant—or Abigail Pierce for that matter! The reminder hardened his resistance.

If he'd learned anything, it was that life could change in an instant. A logging accident had taken him into uncharted territory where his survival was at risk, not to mention his heart. No matter how hard he tried to deny the attraction, Abby was a force to be reckoned with.

He was helpless to do anything about it.

For the first time in his adult life, Jack had to rely on the kindness of others when he hadn't believed it existed.

Abby was kind, compassionate, generous.

If he wasn't careful, he'd begin to confuse that for something far more complicated and dangerous.

At times, the hospital seemed like home, warm and safe; suddenly, it felt like a prison.

Rehabilitation beckoned.

According to the doctors, the treatment he would receive there would restore him to a useful life. *Useful.* No one would tell him exactly what that meant.

Only one thing mattered—getting out of his current predicament and moving on with his life. Suddenly, time seemed like the enemy.

"How long have I been here?"

"It's been two weeks since the accident."

It felt longer.

Another week went by.

Then another.

Before his accident, Jack had led an active outdoor life. Thus, he was in great physical shape, and this accelerated his recovery. His fractured rib healed in four weeks, his arm in five, his leg in six. Each was a milestone allowing him more freedom of movement, but the removal of his leg cast was the big event.

When the cumbersome plaster cast fell away, Jack ignored the white puckered skin, the ugly red scar slashing across his leg at mid-thigh. This was a moment to celebrate—dashed only by the swift but sure realization that he couldn't lift his leg an inch off the bed! It was a crushing blow.

He hid his disappointment behind a careless smile. "Guess I won't be winning any beauty contests any time soon."

"This isn't totally unexpected. Don't give up," his doctor said—as if Jack had a choice. "Once you get into rehab and start working those muscles, you should see some improvement."

"Right." It was either submit to therapy or remain confined to a wheelchair for the rest of his life.

* * *

After the doctor left, Abby was still there, she was always there. He was terrified of growing dependent on her.

She placed her hand against the scar; he wondered how she could bear to touch it, yet he felt her warmth and calm seeping into his bones.

"It's okay, Jack. This is just another phase," she whispered, her voice soft and reassuring, her eyes meeting his, as she bent to kiss him on the mouth.

Jack couldn't turn away. He watched her eyelashes flutter and close a second before her lips touched his. The kiss didn't last long—just long enough to sear his soul.

Nevertheless, he kept his response deliberately light, hiding his reaction to her nearness. This was a first—she'd never kissed him without an audience.

"In case you haven't noticed," he said, "no one's watching."

She looked as confused as he felt. "I know."

Maybe he'd misread the situation, but he was determined to stop things before they got any further. "Abby, you just broke up with Seth."

Her wide eyes puzzled, she stepped back. "What has that got to do with anything?"

"It's a mistake to get involved with someone else so soon." He shifted uncomfortably. "Maybe you think I'm the guy, but I'm not. I could never be what you want me to be."

A small instant shock widened into a hurt pool in her eyes. She shook her head. "I've never asked you to be anyone but who you are."

Jack didn't want to hurt her, but he had to make

the situation clear. ''That's just it—you don't know me. I could never fit into your world.''

''My world?'' she mused with an unreadable smile. ''And where exactly is that? Are you so sure it isn't here?''

Jack only knew one thing. ''This isn't real.''

When she didn't respond immediately, he could feel her tension, but didn't know how to ease it. Did he want to? He'd warned her to keep her distance, so why was he concerned now? She'd kissed him, and he'd told her to cool it.

He'd wounded Abby's pride.

Abby struggled to remain calm, tempted to lash back with a few choice words of her own. ''Thanks for the warning, I'll try to remember.''

Apparently not satisfied with her answer, he frowned. ''I'm glad we agree.'' Shouldn't he be pleased?

Reminding herself that she couldn't attack an injured man, Abby stared back at him in frustration. What did he expect—an argument from her? If so, he was in for a disappointment. She'd agreed, they were mismatched.

Abby left early that day. Fresh snow was falling, but the temperature was above freezing. After being shut in all day, she decided to walk back to the hotel. She needed to get away from the situation. And Jack. But it wasn't that easy. She'd kissed him in an impulse, she'd offered him comfort—nothing more— and he'd rejected her. He was ill, in pain, she shouldn't take his moods personally.

But she did.

She passed the park where some boys were playing hockey on the pond. They kept piling up on the ice, laughing when they did. Smiling at their antics, Abby found a park bench and sat watching them for a while.

Why was she so upset?

The removal of Jack's cast had been disappointing. She'd hoped for some sign that he was healing, but there had been none.

How must he feel?

She had no idea. She wanted to help, she just didn't know how. Jack was entitled to moods, she wasn't. One thing was clear, no matter how he behaved— difficult, impossible and male—she would have to control her own emotions. She sighed—that was easier said than done.

The man did have a way of knocking down her defenses, which was why she'd avoided a more direct confrontation earlier today. She couldn't allow herself to feel anything for a man who wanted so little from her. So, why did his rejection hurt? Abby sighed.

She'd left Jack in the solarium. Now, as if drawn, she looked up and saw him sitting by the window exactly where she'd left him. It struck her that he hadn't been out of that building in weeks. No wonder he was irritable and restless.

Every day she could put on her coat and leave that place. But he couldn't. In his youth, Jack had been locked away for a crime he didn't commit. Had the hospital become another prison?

Abby could only empathize and try to understand how he must feel. Her anger drained away, she lifted her hand and waved. At first, she thought he hadn't seen her; then, after a long moment when she'd almost given up, he waved back.

Yet, despite the token gesture, she felt disconnected. He seemed so distant, unreachable, trapped behind that thick wall of glass.

That image stayed with her.

Rehab. No one had ever asked Jack if he wanted to go there. He'd been assigned, transferred. Like a parcel, he was being shifted from place to place. It reminded him of the dark days after his grandmother died when he was placed in foster care. Everything he'd owned had fit into a plastic bag—the kind people use to take out the garbage.

He'd never forgotten that.

He'd run away.

Now he couldn't run.

Jack's transfer to rehab was an important milestone. Another one. Efficient as usual, Abby had packed his things.

Seated in a wheelchair, which he was still learning to operate, Jack cradled his cactus plant in his left arm. Odd, he'd grown fond of the ugly thing. But then, he had nothing else to cling to, and a prickly cactus was better than nothing at all.

Abby was at his side—but distant, and he had no one to blame for that but himself. Well, things were bound to start looking up now that he was one step closer to getting out and on with his life. Rehab was the last step.

He didn't want to blow it.

His curiosity up, he looked around with interest. The entire building was all on one floor. They entered what resembled the lobby of a plush resort hotel, complete with floral couches and flower arrangements, all in muted colors, sage green and mauve with touches of blue and gold. It was crowded with patients and visitors. Easy to tell them apart.

Then there was the staff.

An attractive blond woman noticed their arrival and broke away from a small cluster of patients.

She held out her hand to Jack. "Hi, I've been expecting you. My name is Michelle. I'm your physical therapist and I've been assigned to manage your case." She was petite, dressed in a loose-fitting blue uniform, practical cotton slacks and a top. "Welcome."

"Thanks."

The woman simply smiled at his terse response and turned to Abby. "And you must be Jack's wife."

Jack enjoyed watching Abby squirm at the title. So, she didn't enjoy being part of a farcical marriage any more than he did. Nevertheless, she recovered her poise with admirable ease.

"Yes, that's correct," she said. "It's good to be here at last. I know Jack's certainly been looking forward to this day. Haven't you, Jack?"

Prodded into a reluctant admission, Jack said, "Right."

He'd been looking forward to this day with dread and anticipation. Reality was likely somewhere in between the two extremes. Entering rehab was like landing on another planet. He was anonymous. No one cared about his past—who he was, where he'd come from, or where he was going when he left. There was just here and now. And the fact that his body needed repairs. He was a case number. Nothing else was real. That included his marriage to Abby, which would end with no regrets on either side the day he walked out of this place—surprising how often he had to keep reminding himself of that fact.

Abby looked so sincere. Was it all an act?

The therapist was speaking to her. "I'm counting on you to act as Jack's coach. The majority of our patients seem to do better when a family member is involved. We try to encourage that whenever it's possible."

Abby's eyes lit up with interest. "I'd love to help any way I can. Just aim me in the right direction."

Michelle smiled, openly approving Abby's enthusiasm. "Great." She turned to Jack. "I'll show you to your room."

She motioned them through a set of wide doors separating the visitors' lobby from the residential area. The doors swung shut behind them. Jack found himself navigating a long wide corridor, a hectic crowded thoroughfare with people moving about in wheelchairs, on walkers and crutches.

Michelle went ahead, pointing out, "—an indoor swimming pool, a whirlpool room, a recreation room with a big-screen television set. There's also a piano."

Jack tried to keep pace with her, but apparently he wasn't fast enough. When he bumped into a second wheelchair, she took control of his chair. He apologized.

"That's okay. Please don't worry about it." Michelle whisked him down one hall after another.

They all seemed long, he'd never find his way out of this place. "With practice, you'll get better at maneuvering a wheelchair in tight places," she assured him when he expressed his concern.

Jack said nothing. He didn't want to get better at operating a wheelchair, he wanted to walk. Abby was curiously silent; he wondered what she was thinking. As a matter of fact, he spent far too much time wondering about that. He tried to ignore her.

Fat chance.

She was wearing her hair up today. He liked it down. Nevertheless, she looked elegant, tastefully dressed in a white silk shirt and black slacks. A colorful scarf in shades of green and turquoise softened the tailored look. Fine tendrils teased the nape of her neck. Her peach-toned skin looked soft and silky. It was probably like that all over. He clenched his hands, they were calloused and rough from years of physical labor. No, there was nothing soft about him. It was all the protection he had.

Abruptly, they turned a corner into a room. His room.

For now.

He'd lived much of his life in temporary rooms. Not one had had a sign of ownership. Before Christmas, he'd used some of the money he'd been saving for years to buy some acreage.

The property came complete with an abandoned

barn and an old stone farmhouse, a fixer-upper. The farm had fallen on hard times in recent years. The idea of salvaging the place had appealed to Jack. Among other things, the roof leaked. The place had probably caved in by now. So much for putting down roots.

"I hope you'll be comfortable here," the therapist said, bringing his chair to a neat stop in the middle of a large square room. Tall windows with a southern exposure made up an entire wall. The room had a view.

Jack remained silent.

"It's a wonderful room," Abby said, typically trying to look at the bright side. "Don't you agree, Jack?"

Jack looked around. Okay. It was larger than his hospital room. It had a closet. And a dresser. But it was still an institution, four walls and a ceiling with only one exit. With a frown, he set his plant on the windowsill where it would get some sun. At least there were no bars on the window. "It will do."

At his lack of enthusiasm, Abby's face fell with visible disappointment. What did she expect from him? He couldn't manufacture an emotion he didn't feel.

When Michelle said, "Well, I guess that's enough excitement for today. I'll see you tomorrow, Jack," all he felt was relief.

When she added, "Abby, if you could come with me and fill out some of your husband's admission forms—" and took Abby with her, he felt doubly relieved.

The "husband" part grated, reminding Jack of Abby's continued fake role in his life. At the moment, he was in no mood to entertain anyone, particularly Abby. Sometimes he craved her company, at other times it was too much for him to handle. A beggar could look at a princess, but sometimes, he wanted to do more than look.

He wanted to touch and be touched.

After signing the admission forms, Abby used the opportunity to speak privately to Jack's therapist. "I'm sorry. Jack doesn't mean to be uncooperative. This is a big adjustment."

"Please don't apologize. His attitude is typical. He's going through a difficult time. Until he adjusts, his moods will go up and down and probably get worse before they get better."

Abby couldn't hide her disappointment. "I was hoping for better news."

Michelle added her initials to the signed forms and slipped them into a file. "There's only so much medical science can do. That's where you come into the picture. The best way for you to help is to keep his spirits up without allowing him to give up when the going gets tough."

Abby laughed nervously. "Jack never listens to me."

"He will, if you're firm. I know it's asking a lot, but that's what he needs from you." The therapist perched on the edge of her desk and smiled reassuringly. "He's bound to have bad moods. Considering how close you are, that's going to rub off on you. It's going to be difficult. I'd advise you find some way to relieve the stress.''

"If only it were that simple."

Michelle smiled. "Don't forget. We're here to help you as well as Jack. Patients with family support seem to do best.''

A family.

Jack didn't have one of those.

All he had was Abby. "I'll do what I can."

Would Jack allow her close enough to help? And if he did, was that far too close for her own comfort? If she let herself care, there would be no safety net, no going back. Jack would demand everything she had to give. Then there was the stark reality that in all likelihood he wouldn't love her back. At the moment, that wasn't even her biggest concern.

Abby worried that Jack would never make a complete recovery. In that case, he would have to learn to live with a handicap which made this phase of his treatment crucial. People did learn to live fulfilling lives in wheelchairs, Abby reminded herself. The proof was all around her.

If it came to that, Jack would have to make new adjustments. In the meantime, she couldn't weaken and allow him to slow down or give up on his therapy just because the challenge had grown larger, the goal more elusive.

After speaking to Michelle, Abby found her way back to Jack's room. She found him sitting near the window.

He was slumped in his wheelchair, staring out at a

frigid winter landscape. It was snowing heavily, but she wondered if he could see the snow. His eyes had that faraway look he often wore; she wondered what he was thinking.

Feeling?

At times, Abby felt invisible to him.

"You'll need some clothes for working out." She searched for some small talk, something mild and mundane to bring him back to her. "I should make a list."

He grunted some unintelligible sound.

She unpacked and stored his clothes in the closet, folded some smaller items into a dresser drawer. Since he didn't have much, that didn't take long. "Can you think of anything else you need?"

Not masking his irritation, he spun his chair around to stare at her. "I don't need anything."

"There must be something," she argued.

"Socks. I could use some socks," he snapped back.

Abby tightened her lips, but the words spilled out. "Why are we arguing?"

"We're not."

"Why are you in such a bad mood?"

His answer was short. "I'm not."

Frustrated, she sighed. "You're obviously not in the mood for company. I think I should just leave before we both say something we'll regret later."

He smiled icily. "Good idea."

She grabbed her coat, and left without uttering another word. On her way out of the building, Abby passed a sign by the front entrance.

Welcome to Rehabilitation.

Chapter Eight

Jack's irritation was contagious.

Tempted to pack up her things and go back to Henderson, Abby was halfway to her hotel before she realized she didn't want to go there. She didn't want to go home either. There was nothing there for her.

Winter was in the air. A few snowflakes struck Abby's face, shocking some common sense into her. Was she going to give in to Jack's foul mood, or was she going to stand up to him? She was half tempted to go back and give him a piece of her mind! However, the memory of his haggard face and slumped shoulders stopped her.

In any case, she was through catering to his moods. According to his therapist, there was a risk that he could slip into apathy. He needed Abby's understanding and patience. He didn't need her pity. From now on, she was going to fight back.

Starting tomorrow.

Abby pulled the hood of her coat over her head, shoved her hands into her coat pockets, and kept walking. A good brisk walk should clear her head. Brisk! With a gale-like wind at her back, she soon found refuge in a downtown department store.

The store was filled with shoppers looking for mid-winter bargains. Wading in among them, Abby took out her shopping list. She didn't have to look at it to remember socks. So, Jack wanted socks. She tossed several pairs of white athletic socks into a shopping cart, then threw in a couple more for good measure.

Wandering around the men's department, she couldn't resist a few marked-down items, extra T-shirts in gray, burgundy, blue and black, sweatshirts and matching sweatpants and athletic shorts.

While Abby shopped for Jack, she tried to deny that she felt like a wife, imagining him wearing the clothes she'd picked out, selecting colors and textures that would appeal to him and feel good next to his skin. A royal-blue sweater the color of his eyes caught her attention. It felt soft and luxurious to the touch. She suspected Jack had experienced little of either in his life. With a sad shake of her head, Abby added the sweater to her purchases.

In the cosmetic department, she sampled a bottle of musk-scented aftershave, then set it down, deciding that might be going too far. Jack was already irresistible.

And impossible.

After paying for her purchases, Abby walked back toward her hotel. She was almost there when she stopped at a corner light and saw a small craft shop across the street. Perhaps Michelle was right—she needed a hobby.

Besides Jack.

She was far too involved in his daily progress—or lack of it—too absorbed in his life, too preoccupied with every stage of his recovery.

Abby crossed the street, entered the small shop and found the yarn department. The rich colors and soft textures appealed to her immediately. She selected some burgundy yarn, then got distracted by teal green. A scarf made out of it would look good with her gray coat. Then, something else caught her attention.

A large selection of pale pastel yarns were on display. Soft, fuzzy, warm yarn, accompanied by a display of crocheted baby afghans in a variety of rainbow colors and delicate patterns. Abby thought of Olivia's baby and reached automatically for a skein of cotton-candy-pink yarn. Yes, she needed pink in her life.

Although thoughts of motherhood had never entered Abby's head before now, she suddenly found herself envying Olivia. For the first time since Drew had announced the good news, Abby took a moment to fully appreciate the fact that she was going to be an aunt. What if they had a boy? Abby reached for the blue yarn. A vivid image of a blue-eyed black-haired baby boy flashed in her mind. When she couldn't dislodge that vision, Abby dropped the pale-blue yarn as if scorched.

She was definitely too preoccupied with Jack.

Somehow, she had to learn to strike a balance between her needs and Jack's. In time, this interlude in her life would end. When this was over, could they be friends? That was doubtful. Only events linked them together, nothing more. They would go back to Henderson, to separate lives, still miles apart.

"May I help you?" The salesclerk startled Abby.

"Yes, please." Abby recovered her composure. "I'd like to make something out of this yarn, but I have no idea how or where to start."

"That's no problem," the salesclerk assured her. She pointed out a wide selection of instruction booklets. "We have everything for the beginner. With a little effort and perseverance, you can be an expert in no time."

Abby smiled weakly. In her experience, nothing was ever that simple. An hour later, she walked out with several skeins of pale-pink yarn, a collection of crochet hooks and detailed instructions, along with a video for novices.

This time, she made it back to her hotel. Juggling her purchases, she found her room key and fitted it into the slot. The phone was ringing. Abby dropped her shopping bags and reached for it.

A clipped masculine voice washed over her. "Abby? Is that you?" Jack sounded irritated.

She sighed. "Who else would it be?"

In a more moderate tone, he dismissed that without comment. "Where have you been?"

"I went shopping."

"I've been calling you all afternoon."

Abby pulled off her coat, then collapsed on the edge of the bed. ''Did you want something?''

''No.'' He cleared his throat, then admitted coolly, ''Okay, so I was worried about you.''

''I'm fine.''

His voice dropped to a husky note. ''Are you?''

''Yes,'' she whispered, because she wasn't fine at all.

''I may have been out of line earlier.'' To her surprise, he laughed hollowly, admitting, ''Anyway, my grandmother always told me married couples should never go to bed angry.''

Feeling a bit bemused at the turn of the conversation, Abby asked, ''What was her name?''

''Moira O'Connor Slade.''

Abby formed a mental picture of a strong-willed woman with twinkling blue eyes. Staring at his grandmother's ring on her hand, Abby smiled. The small diamond seemed to wink at her. ''She sounds very wise, your grandmother.''

''She was.''

They ended the conversation on that note.

After replacing the receiver, Abby smiled ruefully when she realized Jack hadn't apologized for being rude and difficult and antisocial earlier. He probably thought those were virtues. At one time, his survival had more than likely depended on those traits. She understood all that.

Nevertheless, she wondered if Jack would ever lower his guard long enough to realize that he didn't have to fight her every inch of the way.

She was on his side.

Abby dialed room service and ordered dinner. For some reason, she wasn't in the mood for eating in a hotel dining room where everyone else came in pairs. As difficult as it was to be with Jack for long periods of each day, she felt at loose ends when she *wasn't* with him.

Frowning at the revealing admission, Abby reached for the crocheting instructions and started to read. Soon she was tangled up in pink yarn and foreign terms like *single, double* and *treble crochet.*

A simple chain stitch was beyond her comprehension, and she suspected her tension was all wrong from the start. Her sister-in-law was an expert at every imaginable handcraft. Abby was all thumbs. What brand of insanity had possessed her to think she could do this? After half an hour, she tossed it aside.

After dinner, she picked it up again, wrapped the yarn around the hook and tried once more, determined to master the elusive art of crocheting. She desperately needed a distraction—one that wasn't six-foot-two with a killer smile and a world of hurt in his blue eyes.

The following day, Jack eyed Abby warily when she arrived at the hospital. "Good morning."

She wore a determined smile. "I hope you slept well."

"So-so." Jack wasn't about to bare his soul and reveal his nightly terrors to Abby, who was simply passing through his life on some sort of a whim. He dealt with his nightmares the same way he did everything—alone.

So far, that had worked for him.

Together, they went to the physical-therapy gym—a huge room, with fluorescent lights, high ceilings and bright murals painted on the walls in no particular design—just flashes of brilliant color: turquoise, yellow and red, that reminded him of children's finger-painting.

Jack was going to grow to hate this room, he knew it from the moment Abby rolled his wheelchair over the threshold. Everything attacked his senses.

On the surface, it looked like any ordinary fitness center, but with one major difference—the clients were unfit. Young and old blended into one. All of them, including Jack, were trying to overcome or make the most of diminished physical abilities.

Abby pushed him around the room in a wheelchair equipped with all the bells and whistles. But he wasn't like the other patients; he was going to walk out of here.

Abby looked around, typically searching for something positive. "What a lovely room, it's so bright and cheerful. Don't you think so?"

Jack's gaze fastened on a piece of gleaming metal attached to leather straps—a lift. "Right."

It was cheerful—if you had masochistic tendencies. The equipment was state-of-the-art. A male patient was doing chin lifts.

A therapist shouted encouragement. "Come on, try harder. Another five." A group of onlookers cheered the patient.

Jack's therapist Michelle didn't waste time on pleasantries, but got straight down to business.

"We're going to start you out easy today with just a few minutes on the bars to break you in gently."

Jack didn't like the sound of that. "Sounds good."

Never show fear was his motto. He felt odd, dressed in a gray T-shirt and loose sweatpants—thanks to Abby. He owed her a lot—too much. The debts kept mounting.

"The equipment is first-rate," Michelle said cheerfully as she steered him to his assigned mat. "This will be your work space. Make the most of it."

Why the hell was she so chirpy?

Couldn't she see what a miserable place this was? Didn't she care?

Michelle had a long list of instructions for him, and a pep talk. "Acceptance of your condition is the very first step to recovery. I know this is very difficult, but you haven't lost everything. One door closes, another opens."

Jack didn't believe that for a moment. He assumed they paid her to say that. "If all goes on schedule, how long is this supposed to take?"

She smiled patiently, as if she'd heard that question many times over. "We'll have you on a full exercise schedule in no time. Progress may seem slow at times, but each day will bring you closer to your goals."

"When?" That was all he wanted to know.

"Well, that's up to you," came the stock answer.

Jack turned away. He wanted a time frame. But no one had the answer. Or if they did, they certainly weren't telling him.

Apparently, the woman wasn't about to let him off

easily. "All right, let's start with getting you up on your feet."

That caught his attention. Jack leaned an elbow against the armrest of his wheelchair. "That's easy for you to say." The comment was intended to be humorous, but came out sounding defensive.

Abby came to his rescue. "Do we need to start today?"

The woman smiled in understanding. "That wheelchair will get you around for now, but learning to use a walker will give you greater mobility. Then, you can graduate to crutches. And to do all that, you have to start with the bars."

Jack started to sweat. "You do realize that I can't feel a thing in my left leg." There, he'd said it.

"I realize that," the woman said more gently. "It's on your chart. But you still have to get up and move about."

When he ran out of excuses, she steered him toward the bars. "Your arms can support your upper body and your good leg will do the rest."

He had one *good* leg, one *bad* leg. Whichever way he looked at it, he came up short.

After a few more instructions, she left him in the care of one of the aides. Jack couldn't shut out the panic, he stared at the bars. They stretched endlessly before him. There was only one way out of this place, and he was looking at it. He had to recover the use of his leg. Simply putting one foot in front of the other and learning to walk again might prove to be the biggest challenge in his life.

Abby was there, rooting for him. She'd done so much for him, he couldn't fail her.

Jack leaned all his weight onto the bars, took a small step then dragged his injured leg. He stumbled once, got a grip on the bars and hung on until he recovered his balance.

He was a grown man, he'd survived some rough times. But now, he felt helpless, like a baby learning to take his first steps. Finally, he made it to the end and collapsed into his wheelchair.

Abby knelt beside him, handing him a towel to wipe his damp brow. "Jack, that was wonderful."

Michelle congratulated him. "You did great."

Not convinced any of this was going to work, Jack sighed, frustrated. "Can I go back to my room now?"

"Of course. There's a bingo game starting in the recreation room in less than an hour," Michelle said. "You might enjoy it and it would be a chance to get to know the other patients."

"No," Jack said flatly. He wasn't ready to face facts. What if he wasn't any different from those around him—damaged people—all trying to recover some part of their independence?

Abby said awkwardly, "It sounds like fun."

"Then you go and play bingo," he shot back, hiding his gut fear behind irritability. "I've had enough for now."

Damn it! Now Abby looked hurt.

"Hell!" he said, his mouth tight with the effort not to shout. Fighting an unanticipated wave of self-pity, he gripped the arms of the chair. "Look, I'm sorry."

He *was* sorry—sorry he was here, sorry he'd

dragged her into it, sorry about the whole damn thing. Most of all, he felt sorry for himself.

She said, "That's all right."

But he knew it wasn't.

Ignoring the tension between them, the therapist said smoothly, "Jack, I understand. You must be tired. This is your first day here, it's an awful lot to absorb in one attempt. Things will go more smoothly tomorrow."

He wasn't tired, but it was a way out. "Thanks—" He couldn't recall her name.

"Michelle," she said helpfully, her eyes sympathetic, her voice nevertheless firm when she added, "Tomorrow, you can get started on the leg lifts."

Apparently his therapist was no pushover.

Jack noticed that Abby had little to say on the way back to his room. The hallway seemed longer than he remembered. It was also crowded, cluttered with patients not restricted to their rooms. They were in therapy, they weren't really ill, or they wouldn't be here. That was some reassurance.

He'd made it this far.

The patient in the room directly across the hall from Jack's room greeted him with a wide smile. "Hi, I'm Theo." The fair-haired boy was in his teens, propped up in a wheelchair outside his room. "You're new here."

Jack nodded. "Right, how about you?"

"I've been here a few weeks."

"That's tough."

Theo shrugged. "After awhile, you get used to it. It could be worse."

How much worse could it get? Jack didn't want to know. In any case, he had no intention of warming up to this place—or anyone in it. And that included this boy—Theo.

And Abby.

She turned the chair into his room. Jack didn't have a roommate. Money could buy lots of things—privacy was one of them. Abby was footing the bills. As usual, any reminder of her wealth grated on his pride. The least he could do was be grateful. But it was Abby's money.

And she wasn't his.

He didn't want her to think he needed her. Just so there would be no misunderstandings, he had to make it clear.

"You should consider going home," he said over his shoulder.

She stopped the chair abruptly. "I'm enjoying the break from routine."

Jack spun his chair around to face her. "This is dragging out far longer than either of us anticipated. Don't feel you have to stick around and hold my hand."

"I've already signed up for some volunteer work."

More good works.

The thought reminded Jack of everything that stood between them. For one thing, he was probably at the top of Abby's charity list. When this was over, they'd both go back to a normal existence—separately. He might have put a ring on her finger, but they both knew it didn't mean anything.

The last thing he needed was a wife. His weakened

state made him vulnerable—but not stupid. When
Abby looked at him, he could see the softness in her
eyes—a man could drown in it. He wanted more than
pity from Abby.

While he contemplated that unwelcome bit of in-
sight, she spoke again. "Is there anything else you
need?"

You.

But he couldn't say that. She stood a tempting
twelve inches away. He resisted. "I can't think of
anything."

"In that case, I'll see you tomorrow."

When she breezed by him, he reached for her hand
before she could get very far. "Hey, where are you
going?"

"Does it matter?" She tugged at her hand, but he
wouldn't free her until she answered. She evaded his
glance.

At some point in their dealings, he'd discovered
that hurting Abby's feelings always rebounded on
him.

He ran his thumb over the ring on her left hand,
and wondered what he would do with her if that ring
was real. Haul her into his arms and kiss her sense-
less? His bones ached to feel her close.

"Yes, it matters," he said, regretting their earlier
exchange. "I suppose you're still angry about what I
said in front of the therapist."

"Her name is Michelle," Abby returned with some
heat. "And she's only trying to help you. So am I."

Then, why was he feeling under siege, under attack, waiting for the world to crash down on him?

"Okay, I said I'm sorry. I'm a lousy bastard for not appreciating what you're doing for me. It's just this place." He looked around, hoping for an escape route.

The place had the look, feel and smell of an institution, a place where society housed its rejects. And one way or another, he'd been in too many of those to appreciate the finer points of this one. The only bright spot was the cactus plant on the windowsill.

It had survived another move.

So far.

Abby followed the instructions to the letter, keeping the potted plant sufficiently moist and exposing it to plenty of sunlight even in its dormant stage.

Now she sighed. "I know this is difficult, but I'm not the enemy. I just want to be your friend. Is that so impossible? Because if it is, then just say the word. And I'll go."

She visibly held her breath.

So did he.

It was there—just on the tip of his tongue, but Jack couldn't tell her to get out of his life. Nevertheless, he couldn't beg her to stay. With a careless offhand shrug, he dropped her hand. "You're free to do as you please."

She lifted her determined chin. "In that case, I thought I'd check out that bingo game Michelle suggested. It sounds like fun. You're free to join me."

Fun!

She had to be kidding.

She wasn't.

At the direct challenge, his brows lifted in admiration. He felt rotten. He wanted to climb into bed with her but suspected that wouldn't do either of them any good—even if he could manage some sort of seduction. Why couldn't she simply leave him alone? Because she was Abby, and nothing she did was less than complex. Giving in, he laughed softly, unable to deny a hint of grudging respect. The girl had guts— and staying power.

"All right, you win." Jack allowed only a hint of grudging respect to creep into his voice. He hoped she wouldn't read too much into his acceptance. "Bingo it is."

She surprised him again. "Maybe we'll both win."

And maybe miracles happen.

Chapter Nine

Some miracles happen overnight.

Some take longer.

It took Abby less than half an hour to realize bingo was not Jack's game. He looked restless. Edgy. On second thought, that was typical of Jack.

Nevertheless, she was enjoying herself.

The recreation room was large, cozily furnished with sofas, tables and chairs and occupied by a mixed group of patients. The youth from across the hall— Theo—had immediately attached himself to Jack.

They'd found a table. An elderly woman named Delia had joined them. They were midway through the third game when the teenage boy said excitedly, "Jack, you won!"

Jack looked down at his game card. "I did?"

After glancing up at the call numbers posted on the

board, Abby leaned over to place a red marker on the winning row on his card. "They just called number N-sixty-three." Her voice trailed off when he moved abruptly.

His shoulder brushed her breast. At the contact, he looked up, his eyes dark. They were almost nose-to-nose, mouth-to-mouth. His eyes darted to her lips. Abby felt her breath catch in her throat.

"Do we have a winner?" The announcer's jovial voice pulled them apart. He repeated the numbers.

With a glum face, Theo looked at his losing card. "Some guys have all the luck."

The elderly woman peered over her wire-framed bifocals. "Theo, it's beginner's luck. Your turn will come."

The boy brightened. "So, pick a prize, Jack."

Given a choice between perfumed bath beads, aftershave, or a box of stationary, Jack opted for the lavender bath beads—for which he got a lot of teasing.

With his face reddening, he presented the pastel beribboned bottle to Abby. He apologized, as if he already regretted the gallant gesture, small though it might seem to anyone who didn't know their situation. "I know it's not what you're used to."

Refusing to let anything spoil the moment, Abby hugged it to her, along with another small victory. She'd managed to drag Jack out of his solitude. While the bingo game wasn't a roaring success, it wasn't a dismal failure either.

She glanced down at the bath beads. "This is lovely."

"How sweet." Delia took the words out of Abby's mouth.

When Jack shrugged it off, Abby suspected no one had ever applied that description to him in his entire life. Maybe Jack Slade wasn't so tough. Maybe there was a chink in his armor.

With their audience looking on, Abby took a deep breath, leaned over and kissed him. Wasn't that expected of a wife when accepting a gift from her husband? However, to her surprise, Jack kissed her back. The warm pressure, gently exploring, threw her into confusion. She pulled back hastily, turning away, afraid he'd see the yearning in her eyes. The pitfalls of their situation felt insurmountable. What did it matter if Jack was sweet—or tough? Their time together had limits. It wouldn't be wise to pretend anything else.

The game continued.

At one point, the subject got around to an inescapable topic. Delia looked at Jack. "What are you in for?" She made it sound like a prison term—which was close.

"A logging accident."

She nodded. "Therapy relieves my arthritis. I should be going home any day now. How about you, Theo?"

"A snowmobile did me in. I was going too fast, and there was this stone fence." Theo shook his head, as if he still couldn't believe his bad luck. "I wiped out on a curve and landed in here with a head injury."

Abby wondered if he was connected to the woman

with the yellow yarn. "I may have met your mother. Does she crochet?"

He nodded. "That's her."

"I haven't seen her around lately."

"She had to go home after the first couple of weeks." Theo mentioned a town up north, a distance of a hundred miles or so. "My dad took time off to stay home with my younger brothers and sisters, but he had to go back to work. Guess I really messed things up." He looked confused and lonely and very young.

Abby's heart went out to him. "You shouldn't blame yourself. I'm sure your parents don't."

"I let them all down, my parents, my teachers. At first, I couldn't remember my own name. I'm still learning how to dress myself and walk again. I was going to get an athletic scholarship to college, now I'm just hoping to catch up with all the schoolwork I've missed, so I can still graduate in June."

Apparently, Jack had heard enough. "Listen, kid, you aren't to blame even if you messed up. Sometimes, things just go wrong." He spoke with quiet intensity, obviously from experience. "No one knows why. That's why they call it an accident. Don't look back. Just concentrate on one thing, getting out of here. You'll make it."

Theo blinked, then smiled slowly. "Yeah."

Abby felt deeply touched by the verbal exchange and what it revealed about Jack's resilient attitude toward life. She saw the renewed hope in the young man's eyes. Jack had put it there. Of course, he understood what Theo was going through. Yes, they were all going to "make it."

The question was all a matter of degree. How much courage and adjustment would it take to return to a full, active life again? How full would that life be? And what would happen if the goal wasn't physically attainable? She continued to keep that possibility remote from Jack.

Jack won another round of bingo. This time, he opted for the bottle of aftershave.

Abby didn't win.

The game ended.

The evening ended early, reminding Jack that this was an institution with strict schedules. Waking, eating, sleeping: everything was done by the clock.

Abby saw him back to his room. Jack knew she was only trying to be helpful, but he wanted her to go. He was fighting a battle on two fronts, one was physical and involved regaining the full use of his body, and the other was emotional—his heart was at risk. He was tied to Abby.

The marriage might be a farce, but the attraction was undeniably real. In odd moments, the idea of having a wife had a certain irresistible appeal to Jack.

Abby softened his harsh angles, and soothed away the pain and isolation. However, he worried about growing dependent on all the warm and cozy feelings. If only Jack had something to offer Abby. He had nothing, just a battered body and a checkered past.

But he wanted Abby.

He'd wanted her from the moment he'd set eyes

on her months ago in that drafty, dusty old sawmill. Elegant and cultured, she'd glowed like a rose among common weeds.

Clearly out of her natural element, she'd made him ache just by looking at her. Of course, he'd known she wasn't for him. Still, she'd tempted him. When Jack had learned she was attached to Seth, he'd stifled his disappointment.

Now that was over, and here she was, semi-attached to Jack while he was undergoing treatment. Ah, and there was the catch. Getting well meant losing Abby.

Jack felt tense when she asked, "Do you need help getting ready for bed?"

"The nurse will be along." He removed his sweater, pulling it off over his head. He was wearing a T-shirt underneath.

Unaware of his mood, Abby reached to smooth down his hair, fingering the dark thick strands. "You need a haircut." She enjoyed the rich texture. Actually, she liked his hair long. It was starting to curl around his ears.

Grabbing her wrist, he pulled her hand away. His eyes darkened as they snared hers. "A word of warning, Abby. I may be stuck in this wheelchair, but I'm not a eunuch. Don't play games. Don't run your fingers through my hair unless you intend to do a whole lot more."

Her face flamed with embarrassment. "Oh."

"Exactly," he said dryly.

Genuinely curious, she tilted her head, pretending

a sophistication she didn't feel. "I'm not sure if I should be flattered or alarmed."

He raised an eyebrow. "While you're deciding, hands off. Okay?" Was that a promise or a threat?

"Is this necessary?"

"Rule number one—no casual displays of affection when we're alone."

She smiled warily. "Don't you think that's a little extreme? I mean—"

His mouth tightened. "Do you agree or disagree?"

She nodded, speechless. He was serious. He'd warned her not to invade his personal space. He'd also succeeded in making her totally aware of him. Was that his ultimate objective? If so, he'd succeeded. Being tied to Jack Slade was like dancing barefoot in a ring of fire. Exciting but infinitely dangerous. One misstep and she'd self-destruct.

Abby hid that new worry behind a cool reserved smile. "Of course, I agree." No touching, no kissing. That shouldn't be all that difficult to remember.

To her relief, he visibly relaxed, easing the combustible tension that had flared between them.

Like a match set to tinder, they could go up in flames together. He wanted her. That was obvious. In recent weeks, she'd felt the sexual tension from time to time, but she'd ignored it. Now there was no running away from reality. Though controlled, it was there in his eyes.

Jack regretted starting this conversation. In the last couple of weeks, while his body grew stronger, his emotional self-defense system had grown weaker, particularly where Abby was concerned. She'd gotten into the habit of touching him. He knew it was casual, asexual on her part, but once he'd gotten past the crisis trauma stage where every part of his body hurt, he couldn't help responding with a new kind of ache—one only Abby could appease.

He had to put a halt to it before things got out of hand. "Let's agree to cool it."

She flushed. "If that's what you want."

"That's what I want."

Liar.

He tried to soften his words, but they came out hard. "Let's get this straight, we aren't married. I'm not yours to touch and fondle and hug whenever you're in the mood."

Abby gasped. "I wasn't aware that's what I was doing."

Driven to the edge of his patience, he said, "You do it all the time. And we both know why."

"I don't know what you mean."

"You think it's safe, that there's no risk of seduction, that I'm helpless." He banged his fist against the arm of his wheelchair. "That I can't get out of this damn thing."

"That isn't true. I care about you."

His mouth tightened. "Don't say that."

"Even if it's true?"

"What you feel is pity," he argued.

She mocked him with a weak smile. "Please don't tell me how I feel." She picked up her coat. "You can relax, you're perfectly safe from me."

Head held high, she turned to walk out.

So, why didn't he feel safe?

Why couldn't he let her walk out?

Gritting his teeth, he followed her, wheeling his chair out into the hallway. "Abby."

Several heads poked out of the neighboring rooms.

Abby turned back, her face revealing signs of strain and weariness. "Yes, what is it?"

Jack couldn't very well carry on the argument in front of an audience. "It's late, how are you getting back to your hotel?" Though lame, that was the best excuse he could come up with.

Abby looked amazed. And well she should be—it was the first time he'd taken any interest whatsoever in her personal arrangements. He frowned, realizing he had no idea where she went, what she did or whom she did it with when she wasn't here at the hospital.

She paused in the doorway. "I usually walk back to the hotel."

"Is that safe?"

She sighed. "The hotel is minutes away, and the streets are well-lit and patrolled."

He frowned. "If you say so." He didn't ask if she'd be back tomorrow. It was understood. "Do me a favor and call me when you get back to the hotel."

She walked back toward him, her eyes widening as she argued, "Jack, this is ridiculous. I'm not a child. I'm quite capable of taking care of myself."

"Then, humor me," he said dryly.

She smiled tightly. "You sound exactly like my mother."

Jack suspected that wasn't meant as a compliment. "I'd like to meet her one of these days. Which brings up a good point. What have you told your family about us?''

Obviously feeling pressured at the mere thought of confronting her parents with news of what she'd gotten herself involved in when she'd come to his rescue, she said quietly, ''Aren't you forgetting—there is no *us*.''

''True. Thanks for the reminder.''

Abby bit her lip. ''I didn't mean that.''

''Maybe we both need an occasional reminder.''

''You could be right,'' she said.

Finally, they agreed on something!

A soft gleam lit her eyes. He didn't recognize it as defiance until it was too late. She kissed him.

Inwardly Jack groaned. Abby's face was flushed, she looked beautiful, desirable. He wondered what would have happened if they were alone. This was exactly the sort of thing he wanted to avoid. ''Damn it, Abby, we discussed this—''

Her eyes sparkled with triumph. ''I know. You made up the rules, and I didn't argue. But guess what, Jack? Don't look now, but we have an audience.''

By now, they'd drawn a crowd—well, at least five or six.

Exasperated, he rasped the flinty warning, ''I thought we agreed—''

Shaking her head, she interrupted him. ''Correct me if I'm wrong, but isn't this public enough for you? According to *your* rules, that means I can kiss you whenever I please.'' She did exactly that and left him sputtering.

That rebellious spark of bravado carried Abby out

the door and back to the hotel before fizzling out. They'd argued, their first fight, but at least they were communicating.

Assuming his concern had been genuine, she picked up the phone and called him. "I'm checking in to say good-night."

"I'm glad you called." His voice sounded very deep and masculine. "I'm sorry about what I said earlier."

Not expecting an apology, Abby smiled into the receiver. "You didn't mean it?"

He sounded amused. "I did, but I didn't mean to take my lousy mood out on you."

"That's okay. I understand." Abby hung up the receiver. But she didn't understand, not really.

How could anyone know what Jack was going through? Apart from an occasional show of temper, he remained stoic and rarely shared any personal insights with her.

Of course, she hadn't been completely honest either. For instance, he was right—she hadn't spoken to her parents since the accident.

After a moment's hesitation, Abby picked up the phone again, then dialed a familiar number. When a woman answered, Abby took a deep breath and said, "Hello, Mom."

There was a cool pause, then, "Abby," spoken in well-modulated tones. Nevertheless, Abby caught the unspoken note of censure. "How nice to hear from you. It's been some time."

Abby sighed. Her mother had a right to be annoyed. At one time, they'd been close, but Abby was a disappointment to her mother, who wanted her to marry well—meaning up. So far, Abby had managed to avoid that trap. She'd rebelled and moved back to Henderson, safely away from her mother's social circle.

Now, Abby had no idea how to bridge the rift between them and feared it would only grow wider. She apologized. "I've been meaning to call."

"I wish you had instead of leaving me completely in the dark about what you've been up to lately. Imagine my surprise when a friend called to congratulate me on my daughter's marriage, saying she'd read something in a newspaper."

Myra Pierce was a proud woman. Aware that she'd wounded her mother, Abby apologized. "What did you tell her?"

"That it was a mistake, naturally." At Abby's silence, Myra took a deep breath. "It is, isn't it?"

"I wouldn't get married without letting you know."

"How could I possibly know that? Drew eloped. Now you've attached yourself to this man. I once thought I knew you, but now I'm not sure of anything."

"There's an explanation, if you'd care to hear it." Abby explained the mix-up in simple, direct terms.

Myra listened, then said, "I knew no good would come from you going back to Henderson. All I ever wanted was for you to be happy and not bury yourself in a backwoods town like I did."

Abby frowned at this unwelcome revelation. "I thought you and Dad were happy."

"I was, I am—but I wanted more for you. Now you've tied yourself temporarily to this person—"

"Jack," Abby said tightly. "His name is Jack."

Her mother's voice sharpened. "This mistake needs correcting. It doesn't matter what his name is."

"Yes, it does matter. Now, would you like to meet him?"

"If you insist on carrying on with this charade." Her mother bristled audibly. "In any case, I think it's time we got together and had a long chat."

A mother-daughter chat.

Abby knew what those were like. Somehow, when confronted with her mother, she always came out the loser. "Would you like me to drive down there?" It was a two-hour drive to Bar Harbor.

"No, I'll come there. Your father is out of town on business. I'll check my calendar and let you know."

Earlier, a nurse had helped Jack to bed—a reminder of his helpless state. Now he lay awake, recalling every moment of his conversation with Abby.

Could she have any idea what he was going through? Apart from occasional pins and needles, he had very little feeling in his injured leg. That terrified him—whenever he let himself think about it. He'd never discussed it with Abby. He didn't want to worry her. It was uncanny how she'd learned to read his moods.

A top surgeon had repaired his leg, so why couldn't he move it voluntarily? Jack had tried to hide his growing concern until he'd snapped at Abby tonight.

He regretted that, but this was no time to lean on anyone, least of all Abby, no matter how soft and appealing she might seem. He'd warned her off before she could convince herself she was falling for him.

Life had taught Jack some harsh bitter lessons, he knew only one way to survive—he'd had to learn to stand alone.

Now, a youthful voice trailed across the hall, offering friendship, kinship. "Good night, Jack."

Ironically, no one could know what Jack was living through better than this seventeen-year-old kid.

"Good night, Theo."

Other patient's voices echoed up and down the hall until everyone went still and Jack was truly alone. He dreaded the night. Everyone had dreams, but Jack's were nightmares.

The dream was always the same. He was trapped. When he tried to stand, his legs vanished.

A rehabilitation hospital was a hard place to visit day after day. When first exposed, Abby's heart had ached for Jack and all the patients. Since then, she'd grown to admire their courage. Adversity brought out the very best in people—the staff who remained upbeat yet sensitive to patients' needs, the patients who cheered each other on, the families who circled around in support of an ailing parent, child or sibling.

Little things added up. An extra smile, a pat on the back, an encouraging word, a shoulder to cry on—these were all a part of rehab, a world Jack inhabited through no choice of his own.

A world she'd chosen to share.

Nevertheless, Abby wasn't looking forward to seeing Jack the following morning. He'd made up some nonsensical rules to keep her at arm's length, as if she was some sort of man-hungry female set on trapping him. He didn't need a wife. He'd made that abundantly clear more times than she could count.

What he needed was a coach.

Determined to fit that role, Abby turned up in the therapy gym wearing casual jeans and a green sweater. Jack had been assigned an individual spot, a padded gray floormat where he was learning to use crutches.

Despite greeting her with a wry smile, he eyed her with open caution. "You're just in time to watch me fall flat on my face."

She tilted her head. "I can hardly wait."

He laughed. "You're all heart."

She was—but he didn't know it yet.

Theo greeted her with more warmth. "Hey, Abby, watch this." Using crutches, he had difficulty coordinating his arm and leg movements, but he made it.

Theo was among the patients who touched her heart. "That's wonderful." Abby hid her concern behind an encouraging smile.

Theo's youth had been interrupted. While he dealt courageously with his physical problems, he worried a lot about his future. His accident had placed a huge financial burden on his parents. He'd given up on going to college which seemed such a waste.

The therapist called the boy back. "Theo, try that again. This time, try and keep your attention on left foot-right foot."

Michelle then turned to instruct Jack. "Let's see what you can do. Abby, stay with him."

"What if he falls?"

"The mat is thick, he won't get hurt."

Only his pride.

Over the next half hour, each time Jack fell, he picked himself up and started all over again. By the fourth time, Abby wanted to cry, but she couldn't let him see her weaken. When he finally took a break, she released a relieved breath.

"You okay?" he asked.

She laughed shakily. "Shouldn't I be asking you that?"

"I have to be here. You have a choice."

When Abby looked into his bittersweet blue eyes, she wondered if she'd ever had a choice where Jack was concerned.

She was exactly where she wanted to be.

Chapter Ten

A loner and a rebel, Jack had learned to defend himself at an early age. He'd fought his way through life and survived more than his share of hard knocks, most notably a three-year stretch in prison for a crime he didn't commit.

He knew all about betrayal.

When Abby first entered the picture, he'd fought her as well. That situation hadn't changed. How could he lower his guard and make himself vulnerable to her? He simply had no answers. Determined to avoid temptation, he'd warned Abby to keep her distance. To his disappointment, she did.

However, she found other methods to torture him.

Over the next couple of days, while Jack drove himself in physical therapy, Abby volunteered to assist with organizing a dance for the patients.

At first, Abby had thought the dance was a cruel joke.

Michelle corrected her. "You don't have to be nimble on your feet to enjoy music and move to the rhythm. We have a small band, a guitar, a drum and a saxophone, but we're short one piano player. Do you play?"

Abby had found herself involved.

For the occasion, she purchased something new to wear—black velvet slacks and a white blouse lavishly trimmed in lace. The outfit was more feminine than her usual attire and she hoped Jack would approve.

When he saw her, his eyes glowed with pleasure, sweeping over her from head to toe, lingering on soft curves and delicate shadows that drew male to female.

"You look gorgeous," he murmured, taking a position near the upright piano.

Abby felt herself caught in the web of sensual response.

When a few patients arrived, she took her seat, adjusting it to suit her height. "Do you have a request?"

His expression was very masculine. "What can you play?"

If he intended to rattle her, he'd succeeded.

"Anything you want," she said, forgetting her reserve and venturing into dangerous territory.

He chuckled. "I don't think you mean that."

Abby adjusted the music sheet. "What if I do mean it?"

He sobered abruptly. "Cut it out, Abby."

"Do I frighten you that much?"

"That has nothing to do with it."

Testing to see if the piano was well-tuned, Abby played a ripple of soft notes. "Ah, so I do frighten you."

His eyes gleamed. "In any game, someone has to lose. And that someone won't be me."

"What if it isn't a game?"

"Then we're both in big trouble." He glanced around. "I think the rest of your audience is waiting."

Over the next few hours, music filled the room. Most selections were classics, golden oldies, with a few popular show tunes added to the list.

As patients in wheelchairs and walkers took to the floor, Jack didn't participate.

When a dapper elderly gentleman approached Abby and asked her to dance, Abby accepted graciously. Jack watched her float around the room and wished he could trade places with her partner.

Jack wondered how it would feel to hold Abby close. To move as one with her. That thought led to something more enticing. He took a long slow inventory.

Her dark hair was long and probably felt like silk. He could only imagine it against a white pillow. Her skin was pale, peach-toned. She flushed easily. Would she close her eyes when he kissed her long and deep? Or would her eyes darken with anticipation when he touched her? Would she respond? He'd never know.

The music stopped.

Abby returned to her seat at the piano.

The evening had lost its charm for Jack. Like most rehab events, the social ended early.

He was already in bed when Abby came to his room after assisting with the clean-up. The lights were dimmed for the night. A silver moon peeked through the window blinds.

"Oh, I'm sorry," she said, moving cautiously. "I hope I didn't wake you. I left my coat in here earlier."

"I wasn't asleep."

She found her coat on the chair but didn't put it on immediately. "Did you enjoy the evening?"

"Mmm."

At his uncommunicative response, she put on her coat and turned to leave. "Well, I'll just say goodnight then."

Jack's iron will collapsed. He reached for her hand, drawing her to his bedside, damning his lack of mobility.

He wanted to hold her against him. "Aren't you forgetting something?"

"Am I?" Her eyes looked puzzled until she apparently read the heated message in his. She leaned over him, placing her hands on his shoulders.

His gaze fell to her lips, his hands wrapped around her slender waist as he drew her down to him.

He watched her hazel eyes darken to a burnished gold, her eyelids flutter and fall, as if they were weighted. And then he kissed her, feeling her lips part to adjust to his, allowing a soft sigh to escape. He captured it, drawing her deeper into this one small act of possession, perhaps the only one he would ever share with her, because all the fates would never allow her to be his. And yet, the kiss was all the sweeter because it was stolen.

Ignoring all the warning signals buzzing in his head, Jack coaxed her lips apart and tasted her, long and deep, until he needed to draw air into his lungs.

When he released her, she gasped for breath. Her eyes were dark and mysterious, shimmering with promises. No matter how unsatisfactory, this would have to be enough. Despite all his denials, they drew sparks off each other. He'd known it would be like this.

"Jack, I—"

He shook his head. "Don't say anything."

What was there to say? He'd given in to a moment's temptation and kissed her, and now he regretted it. Nothing had changed. Although weakened, the walls he'd built for self-protection were still intact.

Abby turned away, not wanting to see the inevitable signs of hardness creep into his eyes, afraid to hope for any warmth from him. She tried to dismiss the romantic interlude as easily as he did. She'd be a fool to read anything into a simple kiss. People kissed all the time. She'd kissed Jack before, but somehow, this felt more significant.

Obviously, Jack had felt it too—she could feel his tension the following day. Deciding they could both use a change of scenery, she suggested a temporary solution.

"It's a beautiful afternoon, much too nice to stay indoors. How about a trip to the park?"

"It's below freezing." Despite the words, a gleam in his eyes betrayed his interest.

"The sun is warm. We'll bundle up. It will be fun."

More fun.

Like the bingo episode, she simply dragged him into her plan. To her relief, Jack gave in without an argument.

Before he knew it, he was rolling his wheelchair through a set of revolving doors. They went to the park.

Fresh snow lay on the ground and clung to bare tree branches, but the paved walks had been cleared earlier.

He'd gotten adept at maneuvering his wheelchair and only needed help in a few spots where snow had drifted in soft mounds. They followed a walkway around the pond.

Abby remained silent, letting him absorb it all. He breathed in the cold crisp air, felt the sun on his face. There were simply no words to explain how he felt.

He wondered how she knew.

His resistance to Abby was slowly crumbling, like a stone wall eroding with time until it was level and offered no protection from invasion.

Sometimes, being with her felt so right. Even when he knew it was all wrong. He couldn't let himself depend on this flimsy, fleeting emotion. It wasn't real. Sometimes, just looking at her made him weak.

So, don't look at her.

Like a lovesick fool, he looked, drinking in the sight of her dark hair, the fine delicate bones of her face, the elegant line of her body. He felt an emptiness, a hunger for something he'd never tasted.

Dressed in jeans and a long wool coat, with a bright knit scarf around her neck, she looked beautiful, tall and striking, her face laced with bright color from the cold. She walked at his side, hands in her pockets, letting the wind take her where it would. She looked so free.

Free.

Jack wondered where he'd be today if fate hadn't come crashing down on him just as the year ended and another began anew. Certainly not here with Abby.

Before the accident, their paths had crossed but never mingled. They were still strangers, there were so many things he didn't know about her, didn't want to know, if he was completely honest.

It was late afternoon, the sky was high and wide and blue, the breeze felt cold against his face. Rows of maple trees marched along a winding path, their bare branches stark and gray. The pine trees were evergreen and brushed the sky. A couple of blue jays dove in and out of the branches. A gray squirrel scurried out of the path of Jack's wheelchair.

He was amazed at how much he'd missed the simple joy of watching clouds drift by. A gust of wind hurried them along.

Though he was dressed in warm clothing and his legs were covered with a thick wool plaid blanket, he felt a tingling discomfort in his legs. That had to be a good sign. Maybe the electrode treatments were working after all.

Every experience in Jack's adult life had taught him *not* to believe in anything. Nevertheless, he clung to hope. Maybe that was his Irish grandmother's influence, refusing to let him give up when the going got rough. Or maybe that was Abby lending him strength, giving him a reason, willing him to get well.

A youth hockey team arrived to practice on the ice.

Jack smiled when a small dog, a terrier mix, got into the game. Barking frantically, the dog chased the hockey puck from one end of the frozen pond to the other until he caught it between his teeth. Wagging his tail in obvious glee, the dog wanted to play. The boys took off, trying to recover the puck, chasing each other and the dog until they all collapsed in a tangle of limbs and hockey sticks.

Jack's smile became a laugh.

Abby was smiling too. "Are you warm enough?"

"Abby, I'm fine." He tore his gaze away from the skaters and the pond. With Abby seated on a wooden bench, she was at his eye level.

"Do you have a favorite pro team?" Abby asked him, refusing to be ignored.

"The Boston Bruins aren't bad."

"Are they having a good season?"

He smiled dryly. "Do you really care? Or are we just making conversation?"

"I enjoy hockey. As a matter of fact, I used to play."

With frank disbelief, his eyes trailed a hot path from her sleek dark hair to her floral patterned sweater and designer jeans worn under her wool coat. "You did not."

She blushed. "There was a pond near our house. I used to beg my brothers to let me play. Evan—he's the oldest—usually objected, but Drew convinced him to let me play."

"Good old Drew," he said dryly.

"Yes, well," she admitted with a rueful smile, "they both got into trouble when I got hurt."

Abby recalled her mother scolding and saying it wasn't a girl's game. Drew had winked at Abby, they'd shared a secret because she'd slapshotted the puck past Evan not once but twice before he stopped her. Evan had always been perfect; Drew wasn't even close—which was probably why she'd always loved him best.

"Unfortunately, I sprained my ankle and couldn't play the rest of the winter. The following year, I was sent to a girl's school."

He smiled. "And your hockey career was cut short?"

"Something like that. How about you?"

For a moment, she thought Jack wasn't going to respond. He never discussed his past. "I grew up in Boston. Every kid in my neighborhood played hockey."

She responded to the opening. "Were you any good?"

"Sure. At sixteen, I was invincible."

Abby didn't think he'd changed all that much. He still had that indomitable spirit. His accident would have broken lesser men, but Jack was still strong. "What happened?"

Regretting his words, Jack sobered abruptly. How

had Abby managed to wear down his resistance? He never spoke of his youth, there were far too many memories. All his boyhood dreams had revolved around getting a hockey scholarship—that was before Gran got sick and he had to work part-time after school to help pay her medical bills.

"My grandmother died and I got sent off to a foster home. End of story."

End of dreams.

But was that really the end?

Jack denied the inviting warmth in Abby's eyes. The temptation to believe in her—to dream again—was too risky. He didn't think he could survive another failure.

Loving Abby could only lead to more loss.

He'd be a fool to think otherwise.

She smiled warmly. "Your story hasn't ended, Jack. It's just a new chapter."

A new chapter.

Jack wished he could believe in happy endings.

Turning the tables on her, he said, "So, what about you? Was your life's goal to return to Henderson and work at the family sawmill?"

"Yes, as a matter of fact, it was," she said, again to his surprise. "With three brothers, I was a real tomboy."

"I can't imagine that."

"It's true. I had no ambition except to be part of the family business. My father had plans for his sons, but he didn't know what to do with a girl. So, he handed me over to my mother, and she decided I needed to go away to boarding school and learn to be a lady.''

"She succeeded."

His response disappointed Abby. Couldn't he see there was more to her than the outer wrapping?

He smoothed his hand down the side of her cheek. "You are quite lovely."

At the soft rasp of his fingertips against her skin, she flushed, unable to hide her response. "Thank you."

With a cynical smile, he dropped his hand. "Don't tell me I'm the only man who ever said that to you. I'm sure Seth must have mentioned it once or twice."

"Yes, he did," she admitted.

But Jack's opinion was the only one that mattered.

The reality hit Abby like a stone in her chest. She'd led a sheltered life where nothing touched her deeply—until she'd felt this helpless attraction to a tough and wounded man who knew too many betrayals. She was totally, helplessly drawn to him.

Could this be love?

That night, Jack dreamed he was playing hockey, floating above the ice. He couldn't stand, couldn't walk, couldn't skate.

In the morning, the sun broke and he woke from the dream, trapped in his bed. The dream was new, but waking up unable to move was the same.

If he didn't regain the full use of his leg, he'd never be able to return to the woods, climb onto a skidder and work for a day's fair wage. He'd never hike the old logging trails, or climb a mountain.

Maybe Drew would take pity and give him a job at the sawmill—behind a desk. He'd never have anything concrete to offer someone from Abby's background. It never occurred to Jack that he might be enough.

Jack looked exhausted the following day.

Abby wondered if he'd slept at all.

Crocheting was supposed to end her preoccupation with the man, but like many of her recent misadventures, her best attempts hit a snag. Needing help, she'd brought it with her that day.

After struggling with hook and yarn for a while, she held up her handiwork for Jack's opinion. "Does this look like a shell?"

He sent a casual glance her way. "It looks lopsided."

"I don't know what I'm doing wrong."

After a few false starts, she'd finally mastered the art of making a chain, then things got complicated. The instructions called for making a shell. It sounded simple—double crochet five times into one loop, skip two, single crochet, skip two, then double crochet five. Repeat. She'd already ripped the entire piece out three times and was trying again.

"What's the problem?"

She had five new rows completed. "Somehow, I keep adding an extra shell to each row."

His eyes held amusement. "You're probably using the wrong turning chain." He took her hands. "Loosen up. You're too stiff, the tension on the yarn should be light and even."

"You sound like an expert."

"When I was a kid, I begged Gran to teach me how." His face flushed with the admission. "At the age of ten, I didn't realize it wasn't one of the manly arts."

Charmed by the boyhood image, Abby didn't tease. "Can you make a shell?"

He grinned. "Sure. It's like riding a bike, you never forget." He put his arms around her from behind to demonstrate.

Abby tried one, then looked over her shoulder at Jack. Their gazes locked. They were extremely close. She'd never noticed the small flecks of gray in his blue eyes. "Like this?"

"Right." He took a deep breath and released her. He raised an eyebrow at the mound of pale pink yarn. "I hate to ask, but what if Olivia has a boy?"

"I hadn't considered that. I suppose I should make a blue one—just in case."

"In case they have twins—one of each?"

"They'd be thrilled. Olivia's always wanted a big family. And Drew wants whatever makes her happy."

It was that simple. Drew and Olivia completed each other. Their courtship had lasted exactly seven days from beginning to end. Abby could never be that impulsive. It seemed to her that love should come with a warning, enter at your own risk.

She picked up her crocheting again. This was supposed to be calming. She was all thumbs with Jack watching her with that dark brooding expression.

As a reminder of all that was wrong—and right—in their relationship, her glance fell on the cactus plant. The plant sat on the windowsill, rimmed by the remnants of a night frost glazing the window. A weak sun peeked around the edges, trying to shed some light into the room. It was spiny, dark green. A few buds had appeared a week ago, but they hadn't blossomed.

Perhaps they never would.

Nevertheless, Jack's room had begun to feel homelike. Besides his plant, Abby had hung a mobile, whimsical stained-glass frogs dangling in front of the window. When the sun caught it just right, bright green glitter splashed across the off-white walls and ceiling. Music played—Native American flutes and soft drums, healing sounds. There was a collection of books and videos. It was all very cozy.

Usually, Abby sat in a large armchair by the window to take advantage of the scant hours of wintry sunlight.

Day by day, whenever she felt tense or at loose ends, her crocheting progressed. She usually left it on the chair near the window with the delicate shell-like pattern spilled over the armrest. The partially completed baby afghan was there the day her mother came to visit.

With no prior warning, Myra Pierce arrived at the hospital one day shortly before noon. She kissed Abby's cheek. ''I stopped by your hotel, but they said I'd find you here.''

Dismayed at her mother's untimely arrival, Abby could only say, ''Mom, I wasn't expecting you. I have to report for lunch duty in less than fifteen minutes.''

Myra smiled at the less-than-enthusiastic greeting. "I thought I'd surprise you. The weather's frigid, but there's no snow predicted, so I—" She stopped mid-sentence, her pale-blue eyes fastened on the afghan. "What's this?"

"It's not what you think," Abby said.

Trancelike, Myra picked up the yarn, clutching it tight. "Abby, is this why you—?" She sat down heavily. "You're expecting a baby."

At her mother's conclusion, Abby was too stunned to speak. Myra looked at Abby's slender waist, then glared at Jack who was sitting in his wheelchair, before turning her full attention back to her daughter.

"Abby, why didn't you tell me?"

"Mom!" Abby blushed vividly at her mother's misguided assumption that Jack would be responsible for any child she might conceive. Why did an image of a baby with Jack's black hair and blue eyes evoke such strong emotions?

Ignoring Jack's soft chuckle, Abby managed to choke out a denial. "I'm not."

Obviously unconvinced, Myra held up the ball of pale pink yarn. "Then, what's this?"

Before her mother could jump to all the wrong conclusions, Abby blurted the news. "It's for Drew and Olivia's baby." The estrangement between Drew and their parents had lasted five long years. Abby could remember her mother's collapse in the courtroom before Drew was led away in handcuffs. Despite all the hurt and disappointment and recrimination, Abby hoped her parents could forgive their son. Perhaps a first grandchild would start a much needed healing process in the Pierce family. She took her mother's hand. "You're going to be a grandmother."

"But why didn't Drew come and tell me?" With the words, Myra's eyes misted with unshed tears of regret. "He never wrote while he was in prison, he never came to see us when he got out."

Seeing her mother's dismay, Abby sighed. "Maybe he's waiting for you to make the first move."

"I wanted to...so many times." Myra lifted her shoulders then let them fall. "But you know your father. He's still so angry and too proud to bend."

Abby smiled. "I guess Drew inherited some of that pride." She had her share as well. "In any case, Drew and Olivia just found out about the baby. They're probably waiting for the right moment to make an announcement."

"We'll see," Myra said, apparently setting her concern aside while she dealt with matters at hand—Abby. She took a deep breath. "Well, we won't go into all that now. My dear, you're looking—" As Myra took in Abby's blue denim jeans, blue turtleneck and pink smock, her eyes widened with disapproval. "Abby, what in the world is that thing you're wearing?"

Despite a moment's empathy for her mother, the habits of a lifetime lingered. Abby found herself feeling awkward and gawky, less than attractive. "It's a smock, it's a uniform for volunteers."

"A pink lady." Jack spoke up for the first time since her mother's arrival. He leaned his elbow against an armrest, clearly enjoying Abby's discomfort.

With a distracted glance, Myra shook her head. "You'd think they could come up with something more attractive."

Jack grinned, eyeing Abby's shapeless form. "I agree."

Apparently unable to avoid him, Myra took another deep breath. "You must be Jack."

While silently observing Abby and her mother, Jack had been surprised by the apparent degree of coolness between the two. "It's good to meet you. Abby's very much like you."

"Obstinate, pig-headed and stubborn?"

Jack laughed, suddenly taking a liking to this woman. Myra Pierce was small and fair while her daughter was tall and dark-haired, but they both had spines of steel.

He spoke frankly. "I was thinking more along the lines of forthright, determined and independent."

Myra was not exactly charmed, but then, Jack didn't expect her to be a pushover.

"So, you're the latest phase in Abby's rebellion. I knew no good would come of her going back to Henderson with Drew."

Abby's mother confirmed what Jack had guessed all along. He was part of Abby's rebellion against the dictates of her wealthy family. He knew all about the Abigail Pierces of the world. He'd run into plenty of them while growing up in Boston. They typically crossed the street to avoid guys like him.

Jack said quietly, "Drew is a good friend of mine."

Abby's mother didn't blink. "Why doesn't that surprise me?"

Abby hastily broke into the conversation. "Mom, this has nothing to do with Jack. Or Drew. Why don't we go down to the cafeteria? We can have coffee before I report for lunch duty. Then, I can meet you back at my hotel."

"You can run along, Abby. I'm sure Jack and I can entertain each other while you're gone."

Although she didn't appear happy about it, Abby had no choice but to leave, which left Jack alone with her mother.

Apparently, Myra Pierce had a few things to say to him. "What have you done to my daughter, Mr. Slade?"

Jack frowned. "I don't know what you mean."

Myra waved a hand. "The way she's dressed, for one thing."

For some time Jack had been aware of the changes in Abby, but he'd refused to acknowledge them.

"Maybe this is the real Abby," he said, slowly coming to that conclusion. "Maybe you never really knew her."

Had he done the same? For months, he'd denied what he felt for Abby, refusing to see past her reserved front to the generous, tender side of Abby.

Myra spoke again. "She's changed. I'm not sure that's a bad thing. She seems happy. Is that also because of you?"

"I don't know."

"She wants to help you and I can see why. I didn't realize your injuries were so serious. Right now, my daughter feels needed. That's important. But a woman needs more than that."

Jack didn't have to be warned—he knew the risks. "You don't need to worry. Abby and I are just friends."

That didn't begin to explain their complex relationship. But how could he describe someone who nagged him, and never let him weaken or give up? Someone who filled his days, haunted his nights and made him more aware of his loneliness than he'd ever been in his entire life?

One day Abby would tire of her pet charity project. Jack didn't need to be told.

But it seemed Myra felt she needed to warn him. Her motherly concern was apparent. "What happens when you leave the hospital?"

"Nothing," Jack said, aware that he wasn't being totally honest with Myra Pierce.

Abby had changed him in some inexplicable way. Sometimes he couldn't recall another life.

Without Abby.

Chapter Eleven

Abby wasn't looking forward to lunch with her mother. Nevertheless, she changed her clothes to something more appropriate and met her mother in the refined dining room of the Victorian hotel. "I hope I haven't kept you waiting."

"Not at all." Her mother raised an eyebrow but didn't comment on the striking magenta silk blouse and matching suede skirt, not Abby's usual style. They ordered lunch from the menu and drank raspberry tea while they waited for their meals. Their conversation was general—at first.

Myra squeezed fresh lemon into her tea. "I like Jack. Does that surprise you?"

Surprised wasn't the word for it. Abby sweetened her tea and stirred. "Yes, it does."

"I must admit he's not at all what I expected."

Abby stopped stirring and set the teaspoon aside. Knowing her mother's approval rating usually came with conditions, she wondered what was coming next. "He isn't?"

Myra lifted her teacup to her lips. "He's badly injured for one thing. I admire his strength—and yours." She looked at Abby as if she'd never seen her before, then slowly lowered her cup, setting it carefully on the saucer. "That doesn't mean I can approve of this situation."

"It's only temporary." How many times had she said that?

"Even so, you've made the choice to stand by him. I have to say I admire that. He obviously needs someone." Myra's face softened, her words revealed heartfelt concern. "Forgive me, Abby, but I'm just not sure that someone is you."

Her mother's opinion shook Abby into an admission of her own. "I'm not in love with Jack," she insisted, "and he certainly isn't in love with me."

"Well, that's a relief. Jack said much the same thing."

At that unwelcome piece of information, Abby frowned. "He did? What else did you discuss?"

Myra dismissed her concern. "Oh, this and that. I'm glad you're both being sensible about this. It's so easy to confuse pity for love. You could get hurt. And so could Jack if he grows to depend on you. Of course, he's bound to be grateful for all you've done for him, but that isn't enough."

"I know all that." Abby stared out the window.

A turbulent river wound around the bend. Parts of

it were frozen, like oddly shaped ice sculptures rising out of the rocks and gray water. She didn't need her mother to tell her they were all wrong for each other. And Jack had agreed.

Why did that feel like a poison arrow piercing Abby's heart? She wanted to deny her mother's words. Instead, she buried her bruised feelings. It was an old habit. As a child sent away to school, Abby had never learned the give-and-take in any close personal relationship. Thus, she craved approval from those she loved, and avoided confrontations—many times at the cost of meeting her own needs. Would she keep repeating that pattern?

Her mother's voice penetrated Abby's thoughts. "Once he's well," Myra said, "how will you know if there's anything more substantial between you?"

Abby tore her gaze away from the drowning river, unable to deny her own fears. Did she want Jack's unconditional love or his gratitude? Could one grow independent of the other, or were they closely entwined? And how could she separate the two?

"How does anyone know?"

"One day, you'll know." Myra smiled gently as she reached across the table and patted Abby's hand. "My dear, don't settle for anything less."

Jack wasn't in a warm welcoming mood when Abby came back. Abby had found him in the recreation room—not that he was hiding out. "Did you see your mother off?" he asked.

Her mother's visit had served as a striking reminder *not* to let Abby get under his skin.

"We had lunch at the hotel first." Abby removed her coat to reveal a silk blouse and slim skirt the color of an evening sky at dusk, a bright shade between pink and purple.

The skirt was short and revealed a lot of leg. She was a constant temptation, hard to resist. Jack's renewed determination to avoid involvement slipped a notch.

Luckily for him, he wasn't alone with Abby.

Theo was on hand. Jack's former nurse, Tammy, had surprised him by dropping in for a visit. They were just sitting down to play a game of cards.

Tammy placed a fresh deck on the table. "What shall we play?"

Abby took a chair. "I know how to play whist."

Jack gave her a mock pitying look. "Whist is for sissies."

Theo couldn't contain a boyish grin. "Right." He was even beginning to sound like Jack.

Jack kept a straight face. He picked up the deck and shuffled it. "How about four-man poker?"

Abby took a deep breath. "Poker it is."

"Winner takes all."

Abby clearly didn't know whether or not she liked the sound of that. "What are the stakes?"

"How about another round of apple juice?" Tammy's suggestion was met with a general groan.

"Ugh!" That was Theo. "How about take-out pizza?"

"Good thinking." Jack agreed. "With the works."

Abby volunteered. "The loser buys."

Jack frowned at that. She was assuming she would

lose; therefore, she would pay. Somehow, that annoyed him. He didn't need Myra Pierce to remind him that Abby gave unstintingly of her time, effort, energy and money.

Jack had been the recipient of Abby's generosity often enough to know how compassionate she could be. She'd fought fiercely to delay his surgery, just as she fought almost daily to keep his spirits up when they sagged.

Nevertheless, there was always this inner restraint and wariness about Abby, as if she was standing back observing instead of diving in and participating in life. Jack admired her dignity, her poise, her reserve—there was nothing fake about any of that.

He wondered what it would be like to penetrate the last barrier. ''Cut the deck,'' he said huskily.

She cut the deck.

During the first round of the game, Jack found himself throwing away some good cards. Abby lost anyway. But she won the second—and the third rounds.

She looked down at her cards. ''I won?''

''You've got three of a kind.'' Jack leaned over and pointed them out. He grinned when she threw her arms around his neck and kissed him. Losing was worth it just to see her win. He'd once warned her that he wouldn't be the loser in this game of pretence they were playing.

Wrong again.

In between games, Theo pulled a white envelope out of his pocket and unfolded it. ''I got this in the mail today. It's an answer to my college application.''

Tammy asked, ''Well, what does it say?''

"I don't know, I haven't dared open it yet." He laughed nervously, then looked around the table. "Even if I get accepted on some long shot, I don't know how my dad can afford to pay for my college tuition. I was supposed to work this summer and earn some of my expenses. Now that's out."

"Open it," Jack said quietly.

"Okay." All eyes on him, Theo tore the letter open, read it…he was silent for a long moment.

Tammy sighed. "Well, tell us, what does it say?"

"I'm in!" The boy looked up with a stunned expression of joy and disbelief. "That's not all. It says I'm getting a four-year scholarship. Some anonymous donor heard about my accident. It covers everything, even a tutor to catch me up on all I've missed before classes start in the fall."

An anonymous donor.

Jack looked across the table. Without being told, he knew who had arranged for the boy's scholarship. There could only be one person. Abby. He grinned. At one time he'd thought of her inherited wealth as a barrier between them, but at the rate she was giving it away, he'd have to come up with something else.

When Theo went to call his folks and Tammy went with him, Jack was left alone with Abby.

He shook his head in admiration. "You certainly are thorough."

She smiled innocently. "I don't know what you mean."

"You thought of everything, including a tutor. That was a nice touch. But why the anonymous bit?"

She bit her lip. "It's better that way. Please don't tell Theo, it would only be awkward."

"How so?"

She shrugged. "Money always gets in the way of friendship."

Her cynicism came as a surprise to Jack, forcing him to recognize how deeply she buried her feelings. He'd learned that harsh lesson in prison. Ironically, that experience had made him strong enough to cope with his present situation.

But that didn't explain Abby's lack of confidence. Apparently she thought people judged her solely based on her money. He wondered where she'd learned that. Didn't she know her own worth as a person?

Early in their relationship, he'd dismissed her as one of the idle rich, but Abby wasn't that easily classified. When she saw a need, whether it was a scholarship or a collection of books and videos, she did what she could to fill the void. There was so much more to Abigail Pierce than he'd first imagined. She didn't just pour her money into a cause, she gave of herself. Somehow, he was lucky enough to be on the receiving end of her generosity.

Admittedly, it would be so easy to take what she had to offer and damn the consequences. But if he learned to lean on Abby, he might never be able to stand alone.

When she rose abruptly, he asked, "Where are you going?"

"To order pizza."

He frowned. "You won, Abby. I'm buying."

"But I—"

Jack didn't know why he was right on the edge of losing his temper—and something else—but he snapped. "For just this once, Abby, don't argue."

An hour later, while everyone ate pizza and celebrated Theo's good news, Jack found himself once again alone with Abby. Seated in a dimly lit corner of the large room, they had a moment's privacy, which was rare.

She'd brought him a slice of pizza and a cola. "I was hoping we'd have a chance to talk. I wanted to apologize for my mother."

Oozing cheese, the pizza was warm, topped with an impressive array of delicacies. The aroma was tantalizingly spicy. Resisting that, Jack said warily, "There's no need."

"I was wondering what the two of you talked about?"

"You, naturally. She's concerned about you, that comes with the job description."

"Mother knows best?"

He frowned at her strained tone of voice. "Something like that."

Abby picked an olive off her pizza. "You might understand my concern if you knew what happened the last time my mother took an interest in my love life."

Abby had a love life? Apart from Seth, Jack knew of no others. How many were there, were any of them serious? If Abby had a dozen lovers, did he really want to know? Wait a minute, he wasn't supposed to care.

Jack swallowed hard. "What happened?"

"I came close to winding up on an extended island-hopping Caribbean cruise with my parents and their friends. And my mother's best friend's son, Edward."

"Does she do that a lot?"

"Mmm. Luckily, Edward found out and warned me."

Jack shoved the pizza aside. At the thought of Myra's matchmaking plans for her daughter, which clearly didn't include him, he'd lost his appetite. "Was that when you went home to Henderson?"

"Yes, I went home. I needed something to do, so I offered to help Drew at the sawmill." She smiled ruefully. "I'm not sure how much I've accomplished there. Anyway, my mother didn't approve then, and she doesn't approve now."

Jack nodded. "She doesn't think we're right for each other. You have to admit she has a good point."

"Of course," Abby said tightly, knowing she couldn't even disagree. What had she been hoping he'd say? Just as she'd feared, her mother's interference had created a new wedge between them. He was suggesting they return to a casual friendship.

Abby wasn't sure that was possible. "And would you like to know what I think?"

"You're obviously upset. Maybe this isn't the right time to go into this."

Abby couldn't stop herself. "I think you're using my mother's visit as an excuse to stop what's happening between us. You're terrified of letting me into your life. You're afraid I might make some awful demand that you can't meet.''

His mouth tightened. ''In case you haven't noticed, you are in my life. I didn't have much choice in the matter, you barged right in and took over.''

She gasped. Though true, his words hit a sore spot—as he obviously intended. ''And you hate that!''

He drew back. ''Maybe I resented it at first.''

''And now?''

''This argument is going nowhere.'' He cut her off with frustrating ease. ''To get back to the main point of this conversation, your mother wanted to know what my intentions are toward you.''

''And what did you tell her?'' Abby's smooth brow furrowed into a deep frown.

Jack wanted to soothe her worries away, instead he frowned back. When Abby looked at him like that, he wasn't sure about much of anything. He wanted to reassure her, but he couldn't. In addition to giving him a clear understanding of Abby, Myra's surprise visit had served to enforce Jack's earlier decision to cool the relationship.

The fact that ignoring Abby was turning out to be more difficult than he'd imagined didn't change anything.

''I told her we were just friends.'' At Abby's searching look, Jack took a deep breath, and released it slowly. ''I'm not sure she believed me.''

Jack was no longer sure he believed it either.

A few days after her mother's visit, Jack discovered that a daily airing was only part of Abby's plan to mobilize him into an active life. Whether he was wheelchair-bound or not didn't seem to make the slightest difference to her.

But it mattered to him. It prevented him from reaching for something he wanted, and that something was Abby.

She sat perched on the edge of a wooden park bench. The sun was in her hair and in her eyes. She'd brought a thermos filled with coffee from a gourmet shop, and croissants stuffed with a mouth-watering blend of crab and cream cheese.

"There's an ice arena in town," she said too casually, which had Jack sitting up and paying closer attention to the conversation. "A couple of semi-pro teams are playing this weekend. The home team is undefeated this season. If you're interested in going, I can still get tickets."

"A hockey game?" he said, nearly seduced into cooperating by the combination of Abby and a winter picnic in the park, but not quite. The thought of a public excursion had little appeal. "Sounds like a lot of trouble to me."

"Not really," she insisted. "I'll take care of the details."

"How would we get there?"

"I checked, I can rent a van."

Jack frowned. "The place will be crowded."

"Well, yes. But that's not a problem."

"The tickets are probably sold out," he said, hoping it was true. He hated the idea of a crowd. The mere thought made him feel claustrophobic, trapped.

"I brought some dessert." She reached into a paper bag and pulled out raspberry tarts with creamy white frosting swirled on top.

What other magical feats did she have in her bag of tricks? She was a dark-haired witch, casting spells. She handed him a tart. Jack ran out of excuses.

Despite the late date, Abby got tickets—she'd probably bought them from a scalper. The staff caught her enthusiasm.

Jack's therapist and a male aide were enlisted.

Michelle said, "We'll need a nurse on hand, just in case."

Abby agreed.

Jack didn't dare ask either of them to clarify that. If he was expected to suffer a relapse or something worse, he didn't want to know about it.

Thus, Tammy was added to the list. "Dress warmly," she advised. "It's an indoor rink, but the temperature will be frigid to keep the ice hard."

Saturday evening arrived. Jack had agreed to go and regretted it almost immediately. It was too late to back out now. Just as he feared, loading him into a handicapped van proved to be a major production. It also pointed out how complicated and confining life could be for someone in his condition. On the drive over, he felt every bump, every pothole in the road.

"How are you doing?" Abby's voice was filled with concern.

They went over another bump. Jack clamped his teeth together. "Fine. How much farther is it to this place?"

"It's uptown, near the university. We're almost there," Tammy shouted back from the driver's seat. "Hang on. We don't want to be late."

Jack hung on as cars and city lights whizzed past him at a frantic pace. With the sole exception of his trips to the park, he hadn't been anywhere in months. By the time they reached the sports arena, he wished he were back in his room, safe and sound. He felt disoriented.

Since the accident, he'd been sheltered in one medical institution or another where everyone was more or less in the same boat. Now, with a fresh look at the outside, he struggled to accept the reality of what his future might entail. The limitations.

According to his therapist, in any major adjustment, first came denial, then anger, then acceptance. Jack had gone through all the stages but the last.

The parking lot was crowded, but they had no problem finding a parking space—in the handicapped zone. Jack stared at the sign for one long moment, slowly absorbing its meaning. He felt as if someone had punched him in the gut.

Why had it taken him so long to face reality?

Someone opened the back door, and ice-cold air blasted him. "Come on, Jack. Out you go," Michelle said cheerfully.

The aide helped him out of the van, then rolled his wheelchair into the cavernous building. Once inside, Jack could feel the excitement. The level of noise was high, bouncing off the walls. There was no time to adjust.

Tammy went ahead, clearing a path for him.

''We'd better get to our seats. The game's going to start any minute.''

Abby pushed his chair up a long ramp to a tiered row of seats. A group of teenagers stepped aside to give him room. Nothing had prepared him for their reactions. There was the initial shock of seeing him—a man in his prime—confined to a wheelchair. The expressions turned quickly to pity before they looked away, avoiding his eyes, as if he was invisible.

Or contagious.

Michelle patted Jack's hand. ''You okay?''

He gritted his teeth. ''Fine.''

Abby said, ''You're sure?''

''Yes.'' He didn't want her pity.

She frowned. ''Warm enough?''

Or her concern. ''Mmm.''

Tammy was right—it was cold.

Abby forced herself to smile. ''This is going to be fun,'' she said, trying to look on the bright side. ''I've been looking forward to this all week.''

Despite the pretence, she knew Jack was miserable. Maybe things would improve once they found their seats and the game got underway. They couldn't get much worse.

They did.

A little boy stared unblinking at Jack's wheelchair. ''Why does your chair have wheels?''

Abby cringed, relieved when Jack didn't growl at the boy. Instead, he said evenly, ''It helps me get around. I hurt my leg, so I can't walk.''

''That's too bad.''

Jack smiled. ''Yeah.''

"How fast can you go?"

"Fast enough."

The boy's mother grabbed him and apologized profusely. "I'm so sorry. Joey, don't pester these people."

"That's okay," Jack said. "He's just curious."

She smiled helplessly. "Yes, he is."

Thanks to Jack's deft handling, the awkward incident passed without further comment, Abby found their reserved seats. Tammy and Michelle were seated at a distance, and the aide met up with a pretty girl—obviously a prearranged date.

The game started.

Jack watched the teams come charging out onto the ice. Arms raised, hockey sticks aloft, they saluted the cheering crowd of spectators. To his surprise, he felt an adrenaline rush. The first period of the game started slowly while both teams warmed to the ice. No one scored.

During the break, Jack became aware of Abby's silence. For some reason which he couldn't fully comprehend, she'd arranged all this for his benefit. Maybe she felt more than pity? He couldn't let himself dwell on that possibility.

Apart from Gran, no one had ever gone to any trouble to please him. Now there was Abby. He didn't trust the attraction between them, but he didn't have to freeze her out totally. Despite the awkwardness of feeling like a fish in a glass bowl with everyone gawking at him, the least he could do was pretend to enjoy the game.

The second period got under way. When a puck

ricocheted off the goalie's skate and scored a goal, Jack turned to Abby with a forced smile. "The Ravens are a long shot. Who do you to want to win?"

Abby wasn't fooled. She knew Jack was only pretending to enjoy the game. Nevertheless, she appreciated his efforts. She looked over the teams. The Seadogs wore gray and blue, and the Ravens were in red and black.

"I'll go with the Ravens," she said.

"Sounds good."

During the third period, a Seadog fired a backhander past the Ravens goalie. The game was almost over with a two-goal deficit. Stunning the crowd, the Ravens put everything into a final rally. As the puck shot past the Seadogs' goalie for the third time, the crowd was on its feet—everyone but Jack.

Abby's face was aglow as she turned to him. "We won!"

"Yeah, we won." He'd missed the final winning goal.

But suddenly none of that mattered. When Jack reached for Abby, walls collapsed, or was that the roar of the foot-stomping fans? Jack stopped fighting what he wanted most. Abby. He tugged at her hand, drawing her closer until their lips met.

"Thanks for everything, Abby," he murmured against her soft mouth. With a soft sigh of surrender, her lips parted.

Her surrender? Or his? Or was it mutual?

Chapter Twelve

The home team had won.

Jack was glad he'd been on hand to see the game, but the outing had cost him more than physical strength. By reaching out to Abby, he'd given up the fight. Until tonight, he'd managed to push her away. One kiss had changed all that. He knew it, even if she obviously didn't.

Now what?

The ride back to the hospital was uneventful. Abby couldn't stay, she had to return the rental van. The hallway to his room seemed longer. He was worn-out. His leg ached more than usual.

There was no point in hiding the pain from Tammy who insisted on giving him medication. "Don't argue."

He grinned. "This feels like old times."

"You need a strong woman who won't let you walk all over her. I just hope Abby's up to it."

Jack sobered abruptly. "She is."

"You certainly got lucky there, Jack."

"Right." Could it be that his luck was changing? With Tammy's assistance, he rolled over to his right side. She propped his injured leg on a pillow which eased the ache. "There you go. You look terrible. Go to sleep."

"Thanks." Leave it to Tammy to leave him laughing.

The lights went out.

Exhaustion claimed him.

Jack dreamed he was playing hockey, flying across the ice, scoring goal after goal, with Abby on the sidelines cheering him on. Jack groaned and rolled over.

The pillow under his injured leg slid to the floor.

In the morning, a pale wintry sun greeted him.

He was facing the wall, not the window. He stared at the picture of a lighthouse for a long moment, while deciding if he was asleep or dreaming. He'd gone to sleep facing the window. He *always* woke up facing the window.

As far as he could recall, no one had come in and moved him during the night. His injured leg was bent at the knee. When he tried to straighten it, the joint creaked, like an old hinge rusty from disuse. But it moved.

His leg moved.

Jack closed his eyes, savoring the moment. He had

to tell someone, but for now this was enough. Abby would be thrilled at the news.

Abby.

Last night, he'd kissed her.

But this morning, he had to face reality. Somehow, Abby was all tied up in his recovery, he'd grown dependent on her. Even this first movement was probably due to her. Last night he'd savored her sweetness. Then he'd dreamed of her, being with her. Moving his leg was a major breakthrough.

Was he stimulated by Abby? Or the hockey game?

As long as he didn't get well, she would stay by his side. He could bask in her loveliness and pretend she didn't affect him. He was afraid to take the next step in their relationship. What if she rejected him?

He rolled over on his back, amazed when his body cooperated at will. When he tried to bend his leg again, pain radiated from the weak muscles. Catching his breath, Jack stared at the ceiling. His left leg throbbed with agonizing waves of pain. He should have realized, renewed sensation would mean more pain.

That morning, before Abby arrived, Jack requested a private session with his therapist.

It took a monumental effort, the pain was intense, but he was able to lift his leg off the table.

Michelle shared the moment of triumph. "I knew this would happen. You've worked so hard."

"I haven't always been a model patient. I owe you a lot."

"This is my reward. Abby must be so pleased."

Jack frowned. "I thought I'd wait to tell her."

"But why?"

"What if this is just a fluke? What if it all goes away tomorrow and I'm right back where I started?"

"That won't happen."

"Can you be sure it won't?"

Michelle shook her head. "Nothing's ever a sure thing in this business. But I'm betting on you, Jack. You're a fighter. I wish all my patients were as motivated as you are. Abby's been a big part of that. She's been with you every step of the way."

What could he say? He owed Abby a lot—too much.

"Okay," Michelle said. "I'm going to put you through some new exercises, then order a whirlpool session to help ease your muscles."

An hour later, every bone in Jack's body ached. At the end of their session, Michelle left him with a final thought.

"When you tell Abby the good news, we'll order a bottle of champagne to celebrate. Just don't wait too long."

When Abby arrived at the hospital, Jack wasn't in his room. She went looking for him in the gym.

"He's in the whirlpool bath." Michelle handed Abby a stack of towels. "I was just heading down there, but if you don't mind taking these to him?"

Abby accepted the task, which seemed simple enough, except that the mere thought of Jack combined with a whirlpool bath was a little steamy. "Of course."

Abby found the room. She opened the door to a rush of hot humid air. Relaxing, soothing music drifted over the speaker. At first, she thought the room was empty, but then she saw Jack. He was in a large whirlpool tub.

At the sight of his broad shoulders rising out of the swirling water, Abby caught her breath and forgot her reason for being there.

His eyes were closed, his head rested against the edge of the tub. Abby wondered if was asleep. If so, she didn't want to disturb him. Besides, her nerve deserted her the moment she saw his bathrobe on a chair beside the tub. Perhaps she could just leave the towels.

"Why are you sneaking around?" he asked, his voice amused.

Abby jumped, startled. "I thought you were sleeping. I didn't want to disturb you."

"You do disturb me," he said huskily. "So what are you going to do about it?"

Hugging the towels tight to her chest, she walked toward the tub. "The nurse said you needed some towels." While trying to avoid looking at Jack, Abby lost her footing and nearly slipped in a puddle of water. Her voice unsteady, she recovered. "I'll just leave them—"

He laughed. "Coward."

After the previous evening, she wasn't quite sure where they stood, but fear wasn't on the list. "I'm not afraid of you."

His voice sounded amused. "Maybe you should be."

"Is that a challenge?"

"I don't know. The hell of it is I don't know what to do about you," he said to her complete amazement. "In the meantime, come here."

She laughed nervously. "Jack, what is it?"

She came closer until she was within an inch of falling into the tub with him.

"Want to join me? The water's nice and warm." He was looking at her mouth.

"Something's happened." Closely attuned to everything about him, she could sense it.

"You might say that." Jack paused until he had her undivided attention. "I wasn't going to tell you this soon, I don't want you to get your hopes up in case something else goes wrong," he warned. "I moved my leg for the first time since the accident. I still have a long way to go in therapy, but it's a beginning."

Her eyes filled with tears. "Thank God."

Abby's response was all Jack could have asked for. He caught her just as she tumbled into the water. Or did he drag her down into his arms?

In any case, she laughed into his face. "Jack, this is so—"

Jack didn't let her finish. "Yeah, it is."

He brushed the long wet hair off her face. Their eyes met. And the laughter stopped. Somehow, his hands were tangling in her hair and he was drawing her close until he could reach her lips. He silenced her with a kiss that raised the water temperature several degrees. One hand slipped around her waist. Her breasts pressed against him, he could feel the nipples tightening beneath the thin cotton of her shirt. Warm water, fed by jet streams, eddied around them, small circles growing larger.

His hand drifted down her spine, her hip, drawing her to him in slow aching degrees. She arched help-lessly against him. Jack decided the time for logical thinking was over. He wanted her close, closer. Amazing to feel her breasts against his chest. He teased a nipple through the damp cloth and felt her shudder. He could seduce her. Here. Now.

There was nothing to stop him.

Nothing but his conscience.

Seducing her now would only be a quick fix and would barely scratch the surface of what he wanted from her. Maybe someday, if he was whole and well, he could go to her and they could build something strong and lasting together, a future, but not now, not like this. He wanted more.

He wanted tomorrow.

And tomorrow.

But for now, he kissed her again, letting her down gently from the heated excitement they generated to-gether.

When he released her, her eyes were shining. "What about the rules?" he said half-heartedly.

"What rules?"

He refreshed her memory—not that he gave a damn about rules at the moment. "No contact in private."

She flushed. "Oh, those rules."

Jack met her gaze with frank male appreciation. "I'd be a fool to object. But one word of warning. I won't be helpless forever."

Her eyes were bright. "I'm counting on it."

Ah, woman—teasing, tempting, challenging him to get up and walk, promising heaven if he did.

He groaned. "Let's make up some new rules as we go along. Let's see where this goes. We've got time." That he had plenty of. He was on a slow road to recovery, with a slight detour. He could be falling in love. "There's no rush, is there?"

"No, of course not."

Using a metal bar, he pulled himself out of the water and onto the wide ledge surrounding the pool, then helped her out. They sat there grinning at each other.

Jack shook his head in amazement. "Do you know how crazy this is? You, me, us?"

She smiled slowly. "Not if it's what we both want."

One thing was clear in Jack's mind—he wanted Abby. Who knew where this would end? He wasn't making any promises. Nevertheless, despite the serious risk to his heart, Jack could no longer ignore what Abby made him feel.

Final proof of Jack's improvement came a week later in the therapy gym. The bars stood before him.

Michelle stood at one end. "Okay, Jack, this is it. Are you ready?"

He nodded. "Let's go for it."

His leg had grown stronger—a combination of exercise, water therapy and massage. He grasped the bars with both hands, then pulled himself out of the wheelchair. He frowned in concentration, his brow wrinkled, beaded with sweat at the effort. He put his weight on his good leg, took a step, then his bad leg. Good leg, bad leg. Another step. Each step was tentative at first but grew steadier.

Abby had arrived just in time to see Jack pull himself upright. He obviously hadn't seen her yet. She stood absolutely still, afraid to distract him.

With all the grace of a wounded tiger, he'd overcome pain and self-doubt and despair to walk again.

How could she love him?

How could she not?

At some point, he must have felt her presence. He looked up and their eyes met. She could see the fire and determination in his as he took another step toward her, then another.

With each step closer, Jack watched the wonder grow in Abby's hazel eyes. He wanted to walk into her arms.

He'd lived the fantasy out in his head so many times. There had been so much pretence. From now on, he wanted everything between them to be built on something real.

With every step, the pain grew more intense. He refused to let that stop him. He was upright, walking, and Abby was waiting. Drenched with sweat, aching muscles and all, he stopped a foot away from her.

"Jack," she whispered. "You're walking."

A slow smile grew in his eyes. "I wanted to surprise you."

She laughed through the tears. "Well, you certainly did." Her face glowed with what could only be love. "Oh, Jack, you did it. You did it."

"We did it." He reached for her, searching for her mouth, crushing her against him with a strength he'd thought lost on the side of a mountain.

Abby had always been there for him from the very beginning—goading him, encouraging him to get out of bed and walk again. She'd held his hand when the pain got bad and kissed him better when all seemed lost. Finally, he had to admit that he was no longer alone. Abby cared.

And that scared the hell out of him.

With Jack's dramatic improvement, his days at the rehabilitation center were soon numbered. So were Theo's.

The boy went home first.

On his last day in rehab, his family arrived with some of his teenage friends who were all anxious to get him home. With Theo's face wreathed in smiles, they laughed and filled him in on all the school gossip.

Abby was pleased to see him behaving like a teenager, blushing when a pretty girl talked to him. "Who's the girl?" she asked his mother.

"That's Cindy," Phyllis replied. "He thinks she's special. They were supposed to go to the winter prom—" Her voice drifted off, then she sighed. "Not that it matters now. As long as he continues to get stronger. You and Jack have done so much for him. He thinks you're both very cool."

At the moment, Theo was introducing Jack to all his friends. Jack said something that made them all laugh.

"We haven't really done anything," Abby said.

"You created a home away from home. You have no idea what that has meant to him, and to me when I couldn't be here with him."

"We've both grown very fond of Theo. He's a wonderful boy, but I suppose you must know that. He's been good for Jack. They've formed a special bond."

In truth, Abby had often marveled at Jack's patience, his kindness with the boy. She'd been so wrong about Jack Slade. He wasn't at all what she'd imagined when they first met. He was braver than any man she'd ever known. Honest, even when it hurt. He didn't wear his heart on his sleeve, but that didn't mean he lacked one. He was quick to anger, quick to laugh, slow to love.

"Theo, it's time to go." Phyllis said.

When Theo threw his arms around Jack and thumped his back in a parting hug, Abby didn't even try to hold back the tears. The two had been through so much together.

The boy nodded. "So long, Jack."

Jack said gruffly, "Hey, kid, we'll meet again."

"Right."

Theo didn't forget Abby. Using his crutches, he left his family and friends and came back to give her a rib-crushing hug.

She smiled. "I'm going to miss you, Theo."

He stood awkwardly. "Thanks for putting up with me and everything," he said with a weak smile, obviously trying to hide the depths of his feelings.

"Jack'll miss you too. So stay in touch."

"I will." He started to back away. His family was waiting, the rest of his life was waiting. "Abby, take care of Jack."

Take care of Jack.

That was easier said than done.

Soon, he wouldn't need her anymore.

The orthopedic surgeon responsible for saving Jack's leg flew up from Boston for a final consultation.

After a thorough examination, the doctor smiled with approval. "Everything looks good. I'm sure you'll be glad to put all this behind you. How about checking out of here?"

Jack sat on the edge of the examining table. He wanted specifics. "When can I go home?"

"You'll need to continue therapy for some time, but that can be arranged with a visiting therapist. As long as you have someone around, I don't see any reason for keeping you here." He named a date—a mere two days away.

"So soon?" Jack wasn't sure he was ready to pick up the loose ends of his life. So many things were unfinished, barely begun. Abby. Suddenly, everything was happening too fast.

"Unless you have some objection."

Jack laughed. "No."

"You'll need workout equipment at home, you can buy or lease what you need. Your therapist will give you a list. I'm going to prescribe pain medication…enough to last you a while. I wish I could say you won't need it, but that's not going to be the case.

I'd advise you to use it sparingly, but don't be a mar-
tyr either.'' He stood up. ''Any more questions?''

''I never had a chance to thank you.''

''It's my pleasure. You're my prize patient. As I
told your wife after your surgery, I never expected
you to recover to this extent.''

''I don't understand,'' Jack said cautiously.

''The surgery was in the experimental stage. I
couldn't guarantee we'd get the results we wanted.
Congratulations, Jack, you beat the odds.''

They shook hands before the doctor walked out.
Seconds ticked by. Jack was alone in a sterile room,
trying to understand, trying to make excuses for what
Abby had done.

From the first, she'd apparently known his recovery
wasn't a sure thing. Yet, she'd made him believe it
was. She'd sent Seth home because Jack needed her,
she'd stayed out of pity. There was no other way to
explain it.

With no assistance from anyone, Jack gripped the
sides of the table and swung down into his wheelchair. Abby was waiting to share his news. What had
the doctor said—Jack had beaten the odds?

So why did he feel like a loser?

Nothing could explain away Abby's betrayal.

Jack had once gone to prison because he was young
and stupid and he'd trusted all the wrong people. He'd
vowed never to make that mistake again. Like a lovesick fool, he'd trusted Abby.

Chapter Thirteen

It was midday, the sun was shining.

Shouldn't the sky be gray?

Jack should be elated, he was going home. He wheeled himself out of the examining room. Abby was waiting for him. "What's wrong?" she whispered, apparently attuned to his every mood. In that case, she must have felt his bitterness.

"Nothing's wrong," he said, tight-voiced. "I'm going home in a couple of days."

"But that's wonderful," she said, obviously confused.

"Doesn't that come as a shock?"

"Of course not. I always knew you—"

"Don't give me that," he said harshly. "The doctor just explained that you always knew the odds of my making it this far were slim. I wish you'd let me in on that piece of information.''

Abby's face paled. She didn't even try to deny it. ''Please let me explain.''

''It doesn't matter.'' He turned away from her.

Abby came around and placed herself in his path, forcing him to confront her. ''How can you say it doesn't matter?''

His gaze hardened on her. ''Didn't you think I could handle the truth?''

''How could I possibly know?'' she said, entreating him with her soft eyes and trembling mouth. ''In the beginning, I hardly knew you at all. I wanted you to have every chance to get well. I tried to protect you from the truth.''

''You lied to me,'' he corrected her.

Her explanation, flimsy as it was, only served as proof that she'd felt little more than obligation and pity.

''All right, what would you have done at the start if you'd known the prognosis was so unsure?''

''I don't know,'' he admitted in frustration.

''Don't you see? I couldn't take that chance!''

''That's your version. I recall some discussion about skiing lessons.'' He smiled cynically. ''You knew I might never walk again, much less strap on a pair of skis. You knew, yet you never told me. Instead, you made up all that stuff about knowing I would get well. Was that all a lie?''

''It was a hope, a belief, a wish. A prayer. I refused to give up on you, I couldn't let you give up either.'' She took a deep breath. ''I love you.''

No matter what words she used, Jack didn't want to hear them. "You felt pity. Compassion. There's nothing wrong with that, but let's not confuse that for anything else."

"How could I possibly do that?" she said, clenching her hands. "You've never given me a chance."

His mouth tightened. "I know you're angry, I appreciate all you've done, but that's it. Isn't it obvious that you pitied me and confused that for love?"

With a pained expression, she shook her head. "You don't really believe that."

How could Jack believe in her? How could love exist without trust? Like their fake marriage, their entire relationship was a sham, a diabolical hoax. And love was the biggest lie of all. And Jack had almost fallen for it.

Maybe that's what he couldn't forgive.

He took a deep breath and started over. "Maybe I'm not saying this right, but try to understand, I don't want to hurt you. No one in my life has ever done what you did for me in the last few months. You've been there for me, Abby. Part of me grew to depend on you. I'll always be grateful, but that's not love."

Her eyes grew shuttered. "I see."

He wondered if she did. She looked hurt. Suddenly, he wanted to shake some common sense into her, make her understand that he was setting her free, letting her go for her own good. Why couldn't she accept that?

Why couldn't he?

For reasons he couldn't understand or forgive, she'd kept the truth from him. Abby's betrayal cut deep, far deeper than Jack cared to admit. It hurt like hell! It hurt like the real thing—as though he was losing someone he loved.

But how could it hurt to lose her when she'd never truly belonged to him? Everything between them was built on lies, coincidence and pretence. Nothing was real!

Despite the current state of upheaval between Jack and Abby, arrangements for his discharge and the trip back to Henderson had to be made. That evening, Abby called her brother.

"Jack is coming home," she announced.

There was a pause before Drew said, "Is something wrong?"

"Everything's just fine."

"Then why don't you sound happy about it?"

"I am happy—for Jack. He's just not very pleased with me at the moment." Abby explained the situation, leaving out none of her own culpability. Drew had warned her, along with her mother and even Seth. Could everyone else be right and her heart wrong? "Please don't say you told me so."

"Abby, I'm sorry. Keep your chin up, and don't worry too much. Jack will come around. In time."

"Do you think so?"

"Sure." He didn't sound convinced. "In the meantime, just think of coming home."

Leaving the rehabilitation hospital was bittersweet. Somehow, Abby managed to scrape together enough pride to get through it. She exchanged warm farewells with the staff and patients. They had come to mean more than a support group.

Finally, she went to find Jack.

He was in his room, apparently packing up a few last items. When Abby walked in, he frowned.

She hesitated. "Weren't you expecting me?"

A polite stranger, his glance was cold. "I was told someone would be picking me up."

Abby took a deep breath and started over. "This is the big day."

He put on his jacket. "According to the doctors, I'm on my way to a full recovery—give or take six months to a year."

Without any assistance from her, he heaved himself into his wheelchair. Although he used crutches, his leg tired easily, forcing him to rely on the wheelchair.

"Your doctor gave me some follow-up instructions. He's set up a schedule of therapy sessions starting immediately after you get home and settled."

"Look, I'm going home." His voice took on the hard edge she hadn't heard in some time. "Isn't this where we cut the pretence, and all this devoted wifely concern?"

Abby clenched her hands, slipping them into the patch pockets of her coat. "Of course."

How could they be strangers?

Before leaving, he took one last look around the room. "I guess that's it." He didn't even look at her.

Left behind, Abby stood in the middle of the sunny room. Her heart felt heavy when she saw the stained glass frogs in the window. She smiled sadly. Perhaps they would bring the next patient better luck. She took a last look around and found the cactus plant in the trashcan. Apparently, Jack had tossed it away.

She understood.

He didn't want anything closely attached to her.

She tried to walk away from it as easily as he had done, but she found she simply couldn't.

She rescued the plant, brushing some loose dirt off the thick spikes, and wondering if Jack would ever forgive her for not being totally honest with him from the beginning.

Abby saw passion in Jack, mixed with pride in equal measure. If he loved her, he would forgive her in time. She admired his resilience, his courage, his refusal to admit a weakness. His aggression was tightly controlled, like a wild stallion broken too harshly. She'd hurt him, and now she had to pay the consequences.

Gathering up the shreds of her composure, Abby found Jack in the lobby where a small group had gathered to see him off and wish him well. There was one awkward moment.

Jack had found a special friend in Tammy, his nurse who had tended him in intensive care. "I don't know how to thank you," he told her before climbing into the waiting cab.

Tammy chuckled. "That's easy. You can name your first-born child after me."

There was a long silence.

Abby forced a smile. "It's a lovely name."

Jack said nothing.

They took a cab to the airport.

Jack frowned when Abby insisted on carrying the cactus plant onto the small chartered plane deemed necessary because he wasn't up to a five-hour drive back to Henderson. The flight was uneventful. Jack sat up front beside the pilot.

Abby closed her eyes, pretending to sleep.

They landed at a small regional airport fifty miles from Henderson where a rental car was waiting. Abby drove the remaining distance, taking in the familiar landmarks that always drew her home whenever she left this rugged land.

Fresh snow had fallen overnight, coating dormant farmland stretching for miles and miles. Pine trees grew thickly in the surrounding forests shadowing the highway.

A distant cluster of buildings grew near.

The pretence ended at the town line.

Abby pulled over and stopped the car.

She pulled Jack's ring off her left hand. *Gran's ring.* It had never truly belonged to Abby, that narrow band of gold fitted with a small but perfect diamond. Love was like a stone, Abby thought sadly, a rough-cut diamond dug up from the depths of the earth. It wasn't worth a thing until you polished it. Jack had never given it a chance.

She handed him the ring. "I think you should have this back."

She slipped her left hand back into the leather glove, unable to bear the sight of her ringless hand. Although the ring had been meaningless, she felt stripped and naked without it. The ring had changed her somehow.

For a brief moment, Jack's blue eyes burned into hers, the way a blue flame cuts through steel. "I wanted you to keep it."

Abby curled her hand into a fist. "Thank you, but I can't."

She couldn't read Jack's expression as he stared at the ring in the palm of his hand. Then, with a shrug that could have meant anything, he clenched his hand closed and slipped the ring into his inside jacket pocket.

So it was truly over.

Abby had no regrets. There was no further need for pretence. From now on, they would go their separate ways. For a brief time, Jack's injury had bound them together, and now it was over. Freedom had never felt so empty.

So lonely.

There was absolutely nothing left to say. With only five miles remaining to Henderson, they completed the trip in silence.

Though it was sparsely populated, Abby loved the rugged north country; her family had deep roots here, even though most of them had gradually drifted away. Whenever she left, it kept calling her back.

Downtown Henderson was a drive-by, some official buildings, a few stores. They passed the Pierce Sawmill. It appeared oddly quiet at midday, but Abby didn't stop. She was looking forward to seeing Drew and Olivia, and catching up with all their news, but not yet. She wasn't ready to face anyone.

"Turn here," Jack said abruptly.

Startled out of her thoughts, Abby hit the brakes.

"Here?"

"Mmm. The house is up this road."

A break in the stone fence marked a narrow road winding uphill. Luckily, someone had plowed out the steep driveway.

When the car tires crunched to a stop at the top of the hill, Abby sighed with pleasure.

Buried deep within Abby was the child who loved to run barefoot through the grass, skip stones in the pond and dig for vegetables in the dirt. Winter fires, maple sugaring, spring planting and summer's largesse, followed by the maturity of autumn—she loved it all. For as much as Abby was her mother's daughter, she was also her father's child. His mother had been an adventurous outdoor woman. And that was what called to Abby and made her feel whole. Thus, she felt drawn to the earth and the sky; she longed to return to all the places she loved. She took one look at Jack's house and fell in love.

Although not overly large, the warm gray stone cottage had stood up to the ages. The stone was granite. The roof had a cupola with a weathervane. The galloping horse on top was made of black wrought iron, it spun and spun, going nowhere except with the wind. White shutters and a wood porch could surely use a paint touch-up. A weathered red barn stood several hundred feet away.

Taking it all in with a wide glance, Abby's gaze slowly came back to the house which had to be at least two hundred years old. Battered by many seasons both soft and harsh, it would withstand at least another hundred years.

"It's beautiful," she murmured, trying to align this place with Jack the wanderer, the man who craved his freedom and claimed he wanted "no ties."

Could it be that Jack wanted to put down some roots?

"It's just an old house," he said, but pride of ownership in his eyes betrayed him. "No one's lived here for years. When I first moved in, I repaired a couple of rooms to make them liveable."

Abby stored the information with all the other confusing mix she'd discovered that made up this complex man.

When Jack pushed open the passenger door and managed to get out of the car on his own, Abby came around and handed him his crutches.

"Be careful," she said. "The path might be slippery."

"I can handle it."

Jack looked at the path covered with a light layer of snow and hoped he could make it on his own. He had his doubts, but refused to show a weakness. After today, he would be free of Abigail Pierce. It couldn't come a minute too soon. They could go back to being who they were three months ago, before his injury threw them together.

Jack felt worn-out; his leg ached after being on the road all day, but it felt good to set foot on his own land again. Ironically, his house stood in the shadow of the mountain where he'd almost lost his life. Jack knew he had to face it someday, but not yet.

Not yet.

Perhaps it was cowardly, but he turned away from

that sight and looked up at the house sitting on a knoll. The first thing Jack noticed was the new black shingles and shiny sheet-metal flashing on the roof. For a moment, he wondered if he'd come to the wrong place.

Then the front door opened, people poured out, and he was sure of it. He rocked back in surprise.

Luckily, Abby was there to support him before he fell. He couldn't understand what was going on, then he saw the sign—Welcome Home, Jack—a bright-red banner with bold black letters draped across the front window.

Olivia and Drew greeted him arm-in-arm. Reggie, a co-worker, had brought his large family. Jack recognized some of the Carlisles, and Ramon and Rita Morales. Then there was that girl who worked in payroll—he could never remember her name. And so many others.

It took Jack a long moment to recover.

Meanwhile they all crowded around and pulled him into the house. In passing, he noted a wood ramp for his wheelchair.

Everyone talked at once—he didn't have to say anything, which was a good because he couldn't speak past the huge lump in his throat. "You're looking good," someone said.

"Hey, amigo. You are one tough hombre."

Olivia hugged him. "It's great to have you home."

Home.

Once inside, someone found Jack a chair and a footstool. Most of the furnishings had come with the house in the estate sale. He had an attic-full yet to explore. Friends crowded into the house.

There was food and drink.

He was overwhelmed.

Abby hadn't known about the party.

She was so pleased to see everyone on hand to welcome him home, clearly surprising Jack, who didn't think he had any friends. But it seemed he'd earned everyone's respect.

Not pity.

Was it too late for Jack to recognize the difference?

Drew found her in the crowd. "I confess I had my doubts, but it looks as if you both survived."

Abby smiled. "Who planned all this?"

"Olivia."

"Of course." Jack and Olivia had a special bond, each had survived a less-than-ideal childhood.

Abby's gaze fell on the small Christmas tree on a table by the window, and recalled the one in the hospital the day Jack was first admitted, six days after Christmas. Now it was late March. If Jack thought he could turn the clock back and pretend everything that had happened between them in the past three months was all make-believe, he was welcome to try.

She couldn't pretend. She loved him. And suddenly, she couldn't bear to share the same room without being able to tell him, show him how she felt. Her place was at his side, but he didn't want her there. He'd made that perfectly clear. Maybe in time, he'd forgive her for what he clearly saw as a betrayal of trust, but it was too soon.

She had to leave. "You know, I'm really tired after the drive. If you don't mind, I think I'll just go."

Drew looked at her, concern in his eyes. "Aren't you going to say good-bye to Jack?"

She shook her head. "He won't miss me. Don't let him overdo things, will you?"

"Do you want me to knock some sense into him?"

She laughed shakily. "No, thanks."

"Abby," Drew warned. "You're not his nurse-maid."

"I know," she said, but looking after Jack Slade had become second nature to Abby. A habit she wasn't sure she could break without losing part of herself.

Jack didn't see her leave.

At one point, he looked around and Abby was gone.

So, it was over.

He'd never felt so empty.

In his conceit, had he thought Abby would break the impasse and beg for his forgiveness, or argue with him until she wore down his resistance? He should have known Abby would never lower her pride to that degree.

Chapter Fourteen

Bright and early the following morning, someone knocked at Jack's door. He ignored it. Whoever it was wouldn't give up. With a groan, he opened his eyes to find himself in a room with striped blue wallpaper, dark mahogany dressers and white linen curtains at the long narrow windows.

He was home.

Alone.

"I'm coming, I'm coming." After a restless night, Jack swore under his breath, pulled himself out of bed, grabbed his crutches and hobbled to the front door.

He threw the door open. "What the hell do you want?"

Smiling serenely, a middle-aged woman stood on

his doorstep. "I'm the visiting nurse. You're the first patient on my list this morning."

He snapped back. "I didn't order any nurse."

She whipped out a slip of paper. "It says here that Abby Pierce called Doctor Peterson and he notified me. You're on my daily schedule for as long as I'm needed."

As proof, she handed him the sheet of paper with the request for her services.

Glowering at the signature at the bottom, Jack leaned against the doorframe. So he had Abby to thank for being wakened at the break of dawn, but considering he needed the doorframe to hold him up, who was he to argue?

"All right, come in."

Half an hour later, the physical therapist showed up. Jack was soon bathed and dressed and he'd even had a massage, which should have cheered him up, but it didn't.

Reggie's wife arrived. "I'm supposed to clean your house and cook. I can't stay for the whole day, but I'll leave you some pre-cooked meals to warm up in the oven. One of the kids will come over later and keep you company. If you need anything, anything at all, you have only to ask."

Jack waved her in and went back to bed. Apparently, the only person he wanted to see wasn't on his daily visiting list. He should be relieved, but he wasn't. He missed Abby.

The hell of it was, he'd seen her less than twenty-four hours ago. He'd shut her out of his life so he had only himself to blame. Well, he had to get used to getting along without her—try living without air to breathe, water to drink, or sunshine.

He punched his pillow into a ball.

Of course, he knew where he could find her.

No, he was not going to the Pierce Sawmill!

For the next few days, friends and neighbors wore a path to Jack's door. His firewood was cut and split, his chimney was swept, windows washed, rugs vacuumed, copper polished, clothes laundered and his refrigerator was full to the brim.

He soon lost count of Reggie's kids. Every time he thought he'd met them all, another one turned up. They played checkers, watched videos and chattered. Sometimes, they even included Jack. In any case, he enjoyed their company. Anything was better than being on his own.

When had he dropped his loner status?

"Anything else you need?" his nurse said one day.

"Can't think of a thing," Jack lied.

At the end of the week, he was scheduled for a physical exam at the clinic in town. Since he couldn't drive a car, and his motorcycle was gathering dust in the barn, he had no idea how he was supposed to get there. Perhaps Abby?

He wasn't ready to deal with her. Or his anger and disappointment. In fact, he'd shut those down. Better not to feel anything.

When Olivia showed up, he hid his disappointment.

Apparently he failed badly. As usual, Olivia got to the heart of the matter. "You look terrible. So does Abby."

Jack frowned. "What's wrong with her?"

"She misses you."

"Then why isn't she here?"

"Men!" Olivia shook her head in mock despair. "Haven't you ever heard of mending fences, making the first move?"

"There's nothing to repair."

Olivia sighed.

At the clinic, Doctor Peterson, a crusty old character, checked Jack over. "Well, looks like you're fit. They patched you up good. Darn fool, what did you want to go rolling a skidder down a mountain for, anyhow? Didn't you think that deer was smart enough to duck out of the way?"

Chastened, Jack grinned. "I guess not."

The doctor nodded. "Well, next time, you'll know. Ever thought about doing something besides logging? Now, take farming for instance. You don't want to bother with cows. They're just plain dumb. But sheep on the other hand are a delight. If you're interested, I've got some lambs due soon."

Half an hour later, Jack walked out with a prescription for vitamins, a book on raising sheep and a great deal to think about, which was probably why it was too late to stop Olivia by the time he realized they were at the Pierce Sawmill.

"You are coming in, aren't you?" As a co-owner, she parked in a reserved spot. "Just to say hello?"

It would be rude to refuse.

Jack braced himself for another encounter with Abby—only to discover she was out with Seth Powers.

"They went out to lunch," the girl at the reception desk explained. "I think they were going to the diner."

"But they'll be back?" Olivia asked.

"I'm not sure," the girl said. "Abby left a list of things for me to do while she was out."

Drew came out to greet Jack. "Come in, it's great to see you up and around. I was hoping you'd stop by."

"I can't stay long." Nevertheless, Jack accepted Drew's invitation to join him in his office.

Drew sat behind his desk and motioned Jack to take the empty chair. "How about coffee?"

With a coordinated effort, Jack set his crutches aside and eased into the padded chair. "None for me."

"How about coming back to work? I could use your help in the office for a few hours each day, just until you get back on your feet."

Jack frowned. "Thanks for the offer, but I don't want you to create a job for me."

"That's a relief, because I can't afford it."

"I may never be able to work in the woods again."

"So, what are your plans?"

"I know trucks," Jack said, laying all his cards on the table. He had some money, he'd worked hard at various road construction jobs, lived simply, and scraped and saved since he got out of prison four years ago. "I've got some savings, enough to buy some log trucks. And you've got several in various stages of disrepair idling in the yard."

He now had Drew's undivided attention. "Exactly what do you have in mind?"

"The loggers are always getting behind, waiting for the logging truck to show up. You could sub-contract that part of the business out to me. I could get those trucks on the road and hire some drivers to handle transporting raw and processed lumber for the sawmill, plus working with the independent loggers in the area."

Drew looked impressed. "Sounds as if you've got this all figured out."

"I've had months with little else to occupy me, except thinking about the future."

Drew raised an eyebrow. "Which brings up a point. How are things between you and Abby?"

"Over."

"I see."

Jack knew Abby and Drew were close, he didn't want any awkwardness. "Does this create a prob-lem?"

Drew shook his head. "I don't see any reason why it should. After all, you and Abby are both mature, civilized people."

Moments later, Jack left Drew's office and found Abby with Seth. He didn't feel very civilized. In fact, he wanted to tear the sheriff apart, limb from limb.

Abby was smiling at Seth; her smiled faded when she saw Jack. They exchanged awkward greetings.

Only Seth seemed relaxed. "It's good to see you again, Jack. You're looking a lot better than the last time."

Jack looked at Abby. "I had good care."

Abby blushed. "The staff at the hospital was superb."

With a wry smile, Seth looked from one to the other. "Well, I should get back to work. Somebody's cow got loose and is creating a traffic jam in front of the Trading Post."

Abby hated to see Seth leave.

If she'd broken his heart, he wasn't allowing it to show. He was a fine man, they could be friends, but she didn't love him. Finally, she'd resolved that issue. For years, she'd remained untouched, hiding behind her affection for Seth, and not letting other men get close. But that wasn't love. Her emotional reaction to Jack was different—not safe, and perhaps not viable, but it pointed out the weakness in her relationship to Seth. He deserved someone who loved him heart and soul—the way she loved Jack. At the moment, Jack didn't look very pleased to see her.

Abby sighed. "Well, I guess I should get back to work."

Jack nodded. "I should get going."

Neither moved an inch.

Like a man thirsting for a single drop of water, Jack drank in the sight of her. She was wearing a green sweater, her dark hair tied back with a colorful scarf.

Her gaze lingered on his face. "How is everything?"

Was he supposed to answer that honestly, or did she want the stock answer? He settled for something in between. "Drew and I are working out a trucking deal. We've got some details to iron out. But it looks good."

"That sounds wonderful."

"If it works out," he said.

"Mmm."

Jack ran out of conversation. To his relief, Olivia came back. Apparently she'd accomplished whatever she came here to do—well, maybe not quite.

Olivia smiled brightly. "Abby, you're back. I'm so glad because I was hoping you could give Jack a ride home. I would, but I'm feeling a little queasy."

She didn't look nauseous. In fact, she looked like the healthiest pregnant woman Jack had ever seen.

Jack said, "That's not necessary. I can get a ride."

Abby frowned at her sister-in-law. "I'm not sure if Drew needs me—"

"Abby, I can fill in for you," Olivia said firmly. "Jack, don't argue. You need a ride home, and Abby's free."

Thus, with a little manipulation, Jack found himself alone in a car with Abby. They talked about the weather. Luckily, northern Maine had a lot of it, so that covered most of the trip home. In between words, the tension grew, but there was nothing Jack could do about that.

As they neared his house, his gaze became fixed on the mountain where he'd nearly come to a bad end. It grew nearer and nearer, striking dread into his heart. He'd avoided even looking at the place since he'd come home.

Finally, he knew he had to face it. "Can you pull over?"

Puzzled, Abby glanced around. "Here?"

"There, by the log pile."

When the car came to a stop, Jack managed to get out. Leaning heavily on his crutches, he started to climb. There was a logging road, it was rough, but he kept going. It was something he had to do. Abby followed him in silence.

Despite the emotional distance between them, he could feel her concern. Jack didn't want Abby there, but part of him was grateful for her presence. So what else was new?

The trees towered over him, making him feel small and lucky to be alive. He breathed in the pine-scented air. In slow gradual steps, he made it up the mountain only partway. He couldn't risk his neck to go farther, but this was far enough.

"Don't push yourself too hard, Jack."

"I'll do as I damn well please," he snapped back. His leg ached, he sat on a log, admitting he wasn't as fit as he'd like.

Abby looked hurt. "I only meant—"

He took a deep breath, regretting his harshness, but unable to take the words back. "You always mean well, Abby. But it's not enough." Reminded of all the pretence that stood between them, he stood abruptly. "I've seen all I want to see. Let's go back."

"Can't we talk about this?"

"There's nothing to say."

"Why can't we be friends?"

"Because it won't work. You succeeded, you made me *care*. Wasn't that the word you used? I learned to depend on you, but that doesn't mean I can't unlearn it."

Her soft smile infuriated him. "It's not that simple."

He snapped back. "It is."

She shook her head. "Don't you think I've tried?"

"Hell!" He summed up their situation, then turned and stumbled away.

Moments later, Abby followed; she couldn't see the path through the tears swimming in her eyes. With an effort she held them back, refusing to reveal her feelings to Jack.

When she finally reached the car, he was sitting inside, his expression stoney and grim. They didn't speak again. After that day, Abby took her work home and stopped going to the sawmill.

Jack went to the sawmill every day.

The old place seemed to echo with the ghost of Abby's soft laughter, the warmth of her smile. His heart ached for Abby. He wouldn't have admitted that to a soul—living or dead. Gran would have shaken her head in disgust and branded him the coward of Aroostook County.

And she'd be right.

Abby had found a refuge at Oakridge, her family home. No one had lived there in years before she'd moved back in the fall. The house still bore signs of neglect.

Determined to make some improvements to the place, Abby kept busy, using that as an additional excuse to avoid town and any mention of Jack. That was a mistake.

Olivia dropped by and found Abby crocheting. The

pink yarn was a dead give-away. "Oh my." Eyes wide with pleasure, she picked up the baby afghan. "Did you make this?"

Abby smiled. "Don't look so shocked."

"I'm not—well, I guess I am just a bit surprised."

"While Jack was in rehab, I had a lot of time on my hands. Someone suggested I take up a hobby and this is the result. It was meant to be a surprise for you," Abby added ruefully.

"It's a lovely surprise. I love it."

Her eyes muted gray, her soft, delicate features vulnerable, Olivia smoothed her hand over the soft yarn. "Sometimes it doesn't feel real—the baby and Drew and just everything. I go to sleep at night, and it all seems like a glorious dream. Then I wake up each morning, and Drew is still there."

Deeply touched, Abby gave her a quick hug. "He's so lucky to have you. I'm so happy for both of you."

Olivia set the afghan aside. "I've been thinking about you a lot lately. You've been through a difficult time. And Jack isn't always the easiest person in the world."

"No, he isn't, but I understood." Abby looked down at her ringless hands, then slipped them in her pockets.

"Was it very bad?"

"It was terribly awkward at first. I didn't think Jack would ever accept my help, but then we became friends."

"Then what happened?"

Abby shrugged. "We ran out of time."

"And now it's over?"

"Yes." That admission hurt.

"We've missed you at the sawmill," Olivia said with a troubled frown.

Abby made excuses. "I'm sorry, I've been busy, but I'm so glad you stopped by. How about a cup of tea?"

"I was hoping you'd say that," Olivia said, dropping the subject of Jack—to Abby's relief. "I brought fresh blueberry muffins. They're probably still warm."

Olivia followed Abby through the large formal living and dining rooms out to the sunny kitchen and looked around. "I hate to think of you all alone here."

"It's my home."

"But it's so big." Olivia sat at the round oak table. "Don't you ever get lonely?"

Abby filled a teapot with water and set it on the stove to heat. "I'm used to it."

"Don't get too used to it, Abby."

"I know." Abby appreciated Olivia's concern. However, she also knew that if some things couldn't be changed, they had to be endured.

"Jack's special, but I think you know that. He's tough on the outside, but that's just an act."

"Is it?"

Obviously Olivia spoke from her own experience. "He's had a tough life, and it's made him who he is—both good and bad. Jack was awfully young when he lost his grandmother. He had to learn to bury his feelings just to survive. That feels normal to him. Safe. He doesn't believe in love because he never received his fair share of it. And when you don't believe in something, you can't trust it. It's that simple."

Of course, Abby knew Olivia was right. "I have so much respect for the way he's overcome his past. But how do I get through to him?"

"Before anything else, you have to decide if you love him enough to try."

"Love takes two people to make it work." Changing the subject, Abby pointed to the sad cactus on the windowsill. "Maybe you could help me out. This thing is supposed to bloom. I've watered, fed and nourished it. A few buds appeared, then nothing. What am I doing wrong?"

Olivia seemed to know a little about everything. "Some cactus plants bloom at night when no one is watching. You probably just missed it."

What else had Abby missed?

Could she have misread Jack Slade? What if he'd pushed her away when he wanted her to stay? What if she and Jack were so blinded by their differences that they'd neglected to recognize the sameness? Had they failed at love...or had love failed them? Or had they simply run out of time?

Where had she gone wrong?

By not telling Jack the truth, she hadn't trusted him enough to believe in his strength, his courage, his resiliency. Had she seen Jack Slade as weak? Maybe she had.

She'd clearly violated his trust. And for that, he couldn't forgive her.

Chapter Fifteen

Winter still held the residents of Henderson in its punishing grip. Typical for late March, the temperature had dropped below freezing at night, then risen during the day. Dawn came earlier and the sun felt warmer, closer to the earth. It was ideal weather for harvesting sap from maple trees. One morning, the sun didn't come out.

The day dawned heavy and gray with the weatherman predicting at least two feet of fresh snowfall throughout the next twenty-four hours. When it began to snow around mid-morning, the flakes were fat and white, star-like crystals. Sugar snow. Abby watched it fall.

Though fragile and beautiful, the snow was heavy and wet, it could create havoc, bringing down trees and power lines. Abby stared out her kitchen window and worried about Jack. How would he manage alone? Abby turned away from the window.

He was not her problem.

Try telling her heart.

At noon, Abby gave in and called the sawmill to speak to her brother. "I was wondering if Jack had come in today?"

"He's not here," Drew said. "He called in earlier to say he's staying home. Olivia's been driving out there every day to pick him up and bring him into town. He told her to stay put. He didn't want her risking her neck in this weather."

Abby stared at the snow piling up outside her window. "So, he's all alone up there?"

"I know, it's not a good situation. He said he was okay, but his nurse didn't show up either."

"Someone should go check up on him. I think I'll call one of his neighbors." After ending her conversation with Drew, Abby tried dialing several numbers, including Jack's.

All she got in response was a message from the operator saying the phone lines were down in that part of the county. The repair crews were out, but could take days. If the power went out as well, Jack would be without heat. In case of an emergency, he would be helpless.

Abby wasn't under any illusion that Jack would want to see her. Nevertheless, she couldn't ignore the clamoring need to go to his rescue. She dressed in several layers of warm clothes, then filled a couple of boxes with extra food items—just in case they were snowed in for a couple of days.

* * *

"This is insane! You're not going," Drew said when Abby stopped by the sawmill. "The roads are already a mess. They're only going to get worse."

"I'll drive carefully, I promise."

Drew shook his head, saying firmly. "I'm closing the mill down and sending everyone home while they can still get there. You're not driving out there in this weather."

"Of course, she is," Olivia said, equally determined. "Jack's helpless. Someone has to look after him. Abby, did you remember to bring extra flashlights, batteries and candles?"

"Yes, I also included extra matches."

"Blankets, sleeping bags?"

"Mmm."

Drew ran a frustrated hand through his hair. "Does Jack know you're coming?"

Before Abby could respond, Olivia said, "Jack doesn't know what he wants. If Abby leaves it up to him, they'll both be old and gray before he makes the next move. If he has any sense at all, he'll be grateful." She stopped for breath. "Besides, Abby's only going to drop off some food, and a few necessities."

Caught in the middle of a clash of strong wills, Abby felt bemused. "Jack will need food and firewood to last for a week."

"Firewood?" Drew folded his arms, then leaned back against the corner of his desk. He smiled sarcastically. "Going to cut down a couple of trees, are you?"

Abby had made arrangements. "Reggie's going to

deliver a half-cord of hardwood in case Jack's supply is low.''

"So, why exactly are you going to see Jack?"

Abby sighed. "Because he needs someone. I should get going while the roads are still open."

After a moment's hesitation, Drew stopped arguing and tossed her his keys. "Take my truck. It's safer than your car."

Abby clutched the keys in her hand. "Thanks."

"Don't thank me," he said gruffly. "I should be trying to talk some sense into you."

Before she left, he pulled her into his arms. "Good luck, Abby. Jack is a fool if he doesn't appreciate you."

Abby left the sawmill, dismayed to find the wind had picked up with the snow falling at a faster rate.

She had difficulty driving through the snowdrifts. Thank goodness she had Drew's all-terrain truck with four-wheel drive. Visibility was poor, ice kept building up on the windshield wipers. She had to get out twice and clean them off. Knowing she should turn back to safety, she kept going—her only thought to get to Jack.

Jack saw the reflection of a pickup truck coming up the narrow winding road, it disappeared around a bend, then reappeared. The day was gray, the snow heavy and impenetrable. White headlights beamed, piercing the gloom.

He expected the truck to stop at the nearest neighbors, but it kept coming. His long driveway wasn't plowed. What kind of reckless idiot would tackle it?

When the vehicle stopped by the side of the house, Jack recognized Drew's black pickup truck.

Someone climbed out of the truck, then went around and lifted a medium-sized box out of the back.

Then, a wind-tossed figure struggled up the path. Jack threw the door open—only to find Abby.

His heart did a little Irish jig in his chest.

Jack squashed that feeling, hiding his pleasure at the sight of her behind a gruff unwelcoming exterior—afraid to weaken and claim what he so desperately wanted.

But God—he'd missed her!

She'd turned him into a pathetic weakling with needs and feelings he couldn't begin to communicate.

So, he glared at her—as if it was all her fault. In a way it was, he'd never asked her to come to his rescue three months ago. Now here she was again. In his experience, people bailed out when the going got rough, but not Abby.

"You picked a bad time to come visiting," he said.

Breathless, she dropped the box just inside the door. "I thought you might need a few things, just in case you get snowed in for a few days."

"You needn't have bothered. I can manage."

Abby ignored him. "There's more."

Before he could stop her, she darted back out into the storm. While Jack stood by, she made two more trips back out to the truck. On the last, a strong gust of wind created a whiteout, and Jack couldn't even see her, though she had to be less than twenty feet away. He cursed his inability to help. If anything happened to Abby, he'd...

He couldn't finish the thought.

"Abby," he shouted into the swirling blinding snow. The wind whipped around the corner of the house and sent the words right back at him. He stepped onto the porch, catching his breath as the frigid air tore at his lungs. Trying to maintain his balance, he leaned heavily on his crutches.

"Abby! Can you hear me?"

"I'm right here." She came out of the snow squall and climbed the porch steps, laden with a heavy box.

He followed her back inside. "Why the hell didn't you answer me?"

With a startled frown, she dropped the box—it almost landed on his foot. "I did, you just didn't hear me."

A draft came down the chimney, the door slammed shut behind them. Now he was stuck with her.

Abby looked all rosy and flushed from the cold.

Kissable.

Jack tightened his lips, trying to remember why that wouldn't be such a good idea. "I don't know what you think you're doing driving all the way out here in the middle of a snowstorm."

She didn't remove her coat. "I wanted to drop these off. Now that I've done that, I'll be going."

Her hand was on the doorknob when he muttered ungraciously, "You can't go back out in that storm. Any fool can see it's going to get worse, you'll never make it back to town."

"I will if I leave right now."

The prospect of sharing a house with Abby was pure torture. But what could he do? He couldn't turn her out. "Now that you're here, you might as well stay."

"Charming." She smiled tightly at his ill-mannered invitation. "I think I will stay."

She removed her knit cap, shaking her hair into loose waves. Her wool coat came off next. Underneath, she wore a colorful hand-knit cardigan. The deep purple set off her dark hair and fair skin.

She hung her damp outer things on a coatrack.

"I've got a pot of coffee going."

Jack invited her into his living room.

In addition to a plaid couch, a couple of fireside chairs stood on either side of the fieldstone fireplace.

"Coffee sounds wonderful." Abby silently admired the beamed ceilings and wide plank floors. Her gaze settled on the huge fieldstone fireplace. "Would you mind if I started a fire?"

"Good idea." She didn't offer to help with the coffee, for which Jack was grateful.

Switching to his wheelchair to get around the kitchen, he managed to fill and serve two mugs of coffee without any major mishap. By the time he got back to the living room, Abby had set fire to some kindling in the fireplace.

He watched silently as a small flame grew. She leaned over the grate and piled several logs one on top of the other without smothering the kindling.

"There's an art to that," he said casually.

His voice startled Abby.

"Yes." Suddenly aware of his gaze on her, she felt hot and couldn't blame it all on the flames spitting and crackling in the fireplace.

"Careful, the coffee's hot." He handed her a mug.

She took a sip before setting it down on the coffee table in front of her. A collection of popular mysteries were piled haphazardly. One lay open flat on the table, as if he'd just put it down.

Abby attempted to find something superficial to talk about to ease the awkwardness. "Your house is lovely."

"The house needs work," he pointed out unnecessarily.

"But it has possibilities," she responded.

He opened his mouth to say something, then clamped it shut without uttering a single word.

Conversation closed.

So, Jack's house was off-limits—along with his heart.

Nothing had changed.

Abby wondered what she'd hoped to gain by coming here. They were strangers, nothing more, their lives rubbing together but never quite connecting.

Seeking an escape, Abby stood up. "I should get out some candles, store some of the food I brought. Maybe I'll see about getting something together for dinner."

Jack didn't argue.

For the next hour, he pretended to read his book while he watched Abby go back and forth, unpacking the boxes she'd brought. His eyebrows went up at the sight of a lantern and a camp stove. She'd obviously thought of everything.

Abby was nothing if not thorough. He wondered if she made love that way—passionate and intense. And thorough. Having her here was seductive. Her soft floral scent was familiar. Her voice. Her face, so animated when she spoke, so quiet in repose. Her presence filled his senses. While he'd been ill, he'd grown accustomed to seeing her every day.

How could he put all that behind him?

Abby found the kitchen inviting…a rustic collage of wood cabinets the color of butternuts…wicker baskets hanging from the ceiling…colorful rugs scattered on the floor. She warmed up a casserole for dinner. Served with a salad and cornbread, it made a satisfying meal. She dished up some apple pie for dessert.

Darkness fell.

After dinner, small hard crystals struck the window.

"It's icing up." Jack stared morosely out at the sagging power lines.

At eight o'clock, the lights flickered once, twice, then went out. Abby heard the scrape of the chair on the bare wooden floor. "Jack?"

"I'm here."

She hadn't realized he was so close. When she did, it was too late to move out of his way. They stumbled into each other. His hand brushed down her arm to her waist, her hip, leaving a scorching trail of possession before it fell away.

Neither said a word for a long moment.

Abby found her voice first. "I should get the gas lamps out and set them up. I brought candles as well."

"Yes." His voice sounded husky, masculine, aroused.

For a wild moment, Abby thought he might draw her into his arms, she could almost feel the inner struggle he fought. And won. To her disappointment, he stepped out of the way.

While Abby went about the rooms, lighting lamps and candles, she could hear Jack moving around in the kitchen and assumed he was doing the same.

His bedroom was large, furnished with a dark masculine chest of drawers and a double bed occupying a space between two windows. Apart from a few items of clothing tossed on a chair, there was nothing out of place, nothing personal to characterize the space Jack occupied. She knew he'd moved around a lot. Obviously, he traveled light.

Or was he simply trying to find himself?

Abby understood that feeling.

With a shake of her head, she left Jack's room before she started weaving fantasies of being what was missing in his life. When she heard a thump, she went to check in the kitchen and found Jack sprawled on the floor.

With his back leaning against a cupboard, he was rubbing his leg. ''The table got in my way.''

Abby knelt beside him. ''Did you hurt your leg?''

His mouth tight with pain, he shook his head. ''It's nothing, just a cramp.''

''Here, let me help you up.'' Risking another rejection, she reached down and helped him to his feet.

''I'm okay.'' He leaned on her until she handed him his crutches.

''Is there anything I can do?''

He drew away. "There's nothing. I just need to get off my feet for a while."

Abby helped him to his bedroom, leaving the door ajar so the heat from the fireplace could reach. The candles she'd lit cast enough light for her to see her way around the dark shapes of the furnishings.

Jack collapsed on the bed. His face looked white against the pillows. "I think I'll turn in for the night."

Abby handed him a pair of pajamas and left while he undressed. When she came back, he was wearing the bottoms. His bare chest looked masculine, with wiry black hairs and wide shoulders gleaming in the candlelight.

Abby tried to look away, but couldn't. He pulled himself to a sitting position when she silently handed him one of his painkillers along with a glass of water.

"Thanks." He tossed the pill back with the water before handing the glass back to Abby. He rubbed the injured muscle.

When he grimaced with pain, Abby took over and massaged his upper leg. "I've watched Michelle do this a hundred times." Kneading gently but firmly, she tried to relieve his pain. Despite her efforts, the knotted muscle tightened into another spasm.

He groaned. "Abby—" He grabbed her hand and stopped her. "That's enough."

Abby took a deep breath. "But you're in pain. Just relax, and let me—"

He interrupted. "I don't want your help."

For a long moment, Abby just stared at him. He stared back, his mouth set in stubborn rejection.

When would she learn? "I'm sorry."

Despite the dim candlelight, Jack could see the exact moment when her expression closed him out, pretending she wasn't hurt, even when she was. He hated when she did that.

She couldn't hide from him. She wasn't cold, she wasn't *Miss Abigail*. Abby was all spirit and heart. Everything else was camouflage.

He couldn't hide from her. "Don't you know when you're playing with fire? It's not that I don't like you touching me. I like it too much."

As if suddenly made aware of the dangerous state of his arousal, she blushed vividly.

"Of course," she spoke in a reasonable tone obviously intended to soothe him. "You're right. This is a mistake. I should never have come here uninvited. I'm going home."

"It's too late now." He tugged on her hand, dragging her closer. "I can't let you go." He swallowed hard. "Not in the middle of a snowstorm."

She resisted, trying to pull her hand free. "I imagine the road crews are out right now plowing the roads."

He laughed. "Are you going to make me get out of this bed and come after you?"

Her eyes widened in amazement. "You couldn't."

"Don't bet on it." With a hard smile, he tugged on her hand until she landed beside him. His hand found her waist, positioning her by his side.

"Oh, Jack," she whispered on a choked laugh.

He felt her close. "This feels familiar. Have we done this before?"

She flushed. "When you had a fever, I held you during the night."

"I remember. You kept me warm."

"You were delirious. You called me 'Gran.'"

"Did I?"

"Mmm," she murmured.

He confessed, "I've missed you like crazy since I got home."

"I've missed you too. That's why I came."

Suddenly, it didn't matter why she was here. She was in his arms. Jack kissed her, silencing all the questions. One kiss—that was all he intended. But then she ran her hand through his hair and arched against him. She sighed when the kiss didn't stop with just one taste.

Abby responded helplessly.

She felt him shift, taking her with him, until she lay under his weight. He raised on one elbow, looking down at her with a lazy masculine smile.

He found the row of buttons fastening her sweater, freeing them one by one. He smiled at the turtleneck, then the thick thermal underwear underneath. Abby blushed, recalling all the designer lingerie in her closet back at Oakridge. She hadn't been thinking of seduction when she'd set off. Now it was very much on her mind. Her breath escaped in tiny little gasps when he traced the lace edge of her bra.

Jack had always known her skin would feel like silk. He explored further, he ran his thumb across a nipple, and felt it tighten in response. Suddenly, she was wearing too many clothes. He removed them, slowly, achingly. She glowed, naked in the flickering firelight. Soft and womanly, her breasts were cushioned against his chest. Everywhere he touched was soft and warm and wet.

When his leg slid between hers, he felt a sharp pain in his thigh but managed to ignore it. Abby slid her hands down over his hips, removing the last bit of clothing between them, nearly sending him over the edge.

"Jack, I love you," she whispered, her heart in her lovely bright eyes, promising heaven.

"Abby, I need you. Are you sure?"

Her eyes clouded. "Are you?"

"I asked you first." He laughed. Ridiculous to be laughing in bed. Arguing gently. Making love. How did she make everything seem so simple and light? How he wished he'd known her when he was young and foolish and full of impossible dreams....

Another wave of pain hit him. Like mist, his vision of Abby wavered. When everything went foggy, he shook his head to clear it. She was still there. She wasn't a dream. Taking her mouth in a long drugging kiss, he explored the sweetness waiting for him. One taste wasn't enough.

Never enough.

The storm raged outside. The wind howled, trying to find every hollow, crack and crevice to get inside. The snow continued to fall, white and pure over the old stone house, sealing lovers off from the rest of the world. Nothing existed but this magic between them.

He just didn't know the words to tell her.

Chapter Sixteen

By morning the storm had spent its fury and drifted out to sea. Jack woke with Abby in his arms. She was naked. So was he. They'd made love. The hell of it was he was still groggy from painkillers and couldn't remember much about the details. However, all the evidence was there.

Abby's purple sweater was tangled with his blue denim shirt at the foot of the bed. Jack could recall stripping her clothes off inch by inch, feeling her, touching her. He'd felt her willing response, heard her whispered words of love. He wished Abby hadn't said anything.

Unable to come up with the words he knew she wanted to hear, he'd murmured back words of need and want. Now he had to come up with a better response.

He'd satisfied a hunger. Abby deserved more, but he didn't know if he had it in him to love anyone.

Now she was asleep in his bed. As if things weren't bad enough, he took one look at her and wanted to make love to her all over again. She lay curled up beside him, her hair fanned out over the pillow, a vague unreadable smile on her face. With a groan, Jack rubbed his hand over his face.

Trying his best not to wake her, he sat up and pulled on his pants. Then, he reached for his crutches.

Reality hit. He'd made love to Abby. But nothing had actually changed. He was still dependent, she still pitied him. Why else would she come out in a raging snowstorm to rescue him yet again? Did he need further proof?

He had nothing to offer Abby—other than a life with no guarantee of security. He couldn't do that to her.

He'd lingered too long.

Abby woke with the sun in her eyes, and Jack sitting up in bed beside her. She smiled, relieved to find the sheet covering her nakedness. Suddenly, she felt shy where she hadn't felt any inhibitions the night before.

"Good morning." She tried to hide her unease behind a casual pose. This was new territory for her. She'd slept in Jack's arms, they'd shared the night, weathered the storm, but now she felt this coolness. "Have you been awake long?"

Jack shook his head. "Abby, I don't know how to say this. I'm sorry. This is a mistake."

Abby sat up, pulling the blankets tight around her,

leaning back against the pillows. "I'm not sure I understand what you mean."

"You came out here to help, and I took advantage of the situation."

She wouldn't accept that as an excuse. "I thought the decision was mutual."

He frowned. "You deserve a commitment. I have nothing to offer. Nothing but a mangled body and an uncertain future."

"Do you actually think I care about any of that?"

His face darkened. "Maybe you don't. But I do."

She shook her head. "None of that matters, not to me."

While she searched for words, he put on his shirt. "Don't you get it? It would never work."

Abby could see the trapped expression in his eyes. Dealt another rejection when she least expected it, she tried to recover her tattered pride. No matter how Jack tried to disguise the truth of their situation, what he was really saying was that *she* didn't fit into his life.

"I love you," she said with a sad shake of her head. "But there's no rule that says you have to love me back."

"Damn it, that's not what I'm saying." With the harsh words, he grabbed his crutches.

Abby's composure almost cracked, along with her heart. Jack thought all she felt was pity. How wrong could he be? She watched him limp from the room. In her eyes, he stood taller than any man she'd ever known.

Over the past months she'd seen him seriously hurt, flat on his back, then in a wheelchair and now on crutches. Through all of that, he'd remained strong, inspiring others, his indomitable spirit uncrushed. If he couldn't accept her love, then he was right. There was no future for them.

Feeling chilled to the bone, Abby rose. She held the curtain aside, and looked at the snow piled up in drifts around the house. It had stopped snowing.

She could go home.

Abby faced the painful knowledge that their on-again, off-again relationship was finally over. She could no longer pretend that her love would one day overcome Jack's pride, or his cynicism. For months, while he was hospitalized, she'd made herself indispensable, caring for him, hoping he'd learn to love her. But love wasn't a learned response. In the end, all that giving had only left her feeling empty. Why had it taken her so long to wake up to the truth? She didn't want Jack to need her; she wanted him to love her.

After getting dressed, Abby lit a fire in the fireplace, then cooked a breakfast of fried eggs and ham on the portable gas stove she'd brought in case of an emergency. Well, they'd weathered the storm, but not the aftermath. Their relationship felt strained to the breaking point. But time didn't stop just because life had become unbearable.

Over breakfast, apart from a few awkward words, they had little to say to each other. With the sun shining and the snow melting from the eaves, there was clearly no excuse for Abby to remain.

She made no attempt to hide her heartfelt relief. ''The road crews are out.''

''That's good,'' Jack said, piling more stones on the growing wall between them. ''Reggie should be here by noon to plow out the driveway.''

Unsaid words bounced off the walls, creating an unbearable tension. Abby didn't eat much. Neither did Jack. After the meal she escaped to the kitchen.

Unable to bear the agony of one more loss, Jack stepped outdoors onto the porch. He lived in the shadow of the mountain where he was injured months ago. He stared up at the mountain, the sight still haunting him. He'd come so close to dying up there. He could almost feel the coldness creeping over him—the desperation—and the regrets.

Thinking of regrets, he and Abby had made love the night before with no thought of the consequences. What if she was pregnant? Jack couldn't ignore the possibility.

His own father had taken off for parts unknown when his mother learned she was pregnant. She'd died giving birth to Jack. It was history now. But Jack knew that if he ever had a son or a daughter, that child would know it was wanted and loved by both parents from the day it was born. There was no room for half measures, no second thoughts. Was Abby capable of that level of commitment? Of course she was.

For months, she'd given—he'd taken. Last night, he'd taken her again, and held back a vital part of himself.

He cursed himself for walking out on Abby this morning. How could he explain what he didn't understand himself? What if she felt more than pity for him, what if she loved him? Was it such a risk to admit how much he needed Abby? The thought of life without her seemed bleak. Who was he kidding? He wanted Abby.

Jack looked up at the mountain and recalled vowing to do things differently if he had his life to live over, if given a second chance. For one thing, he would reach higher.

He turned at the sound of the door opening and closing. Abby stood there—so unsure. So sad. So lovely. His Abby. This was good-bye. His heart shuddered at the thought.

Abby'd poured him a fresh cup of coffee. She felt the sun, surprisingly warm and bright, almost blinding. It hurt her eyes, but she saw Jack frown as she approached him. She handed him a cup. ''I made a fresh pot. I thought you could use this.''

''Thanks.'' He set the coffee cup on the rail. ''Abby, we have to talk.''

Here it came—the regrets, the excuses, the rejection.

She squared her shoulders. ''Yes, I know.''

His eyes were so blue. She couldn't look at him as he started to speak. She averted her face and stared out over Jack's farm. Odd to think of him—a city boy—owning a farm.

Was that his heart's desire?

Stone walls marked the boundaries of his property. He'd posted No Trespassing signs. The land was hilly with a partially frozen stream. In the spring it would flood the bottom acres, turning it to rich farmland.

A farm girl at heart, Abby couldn't help wondering if he planned to grow anything productive there. Or would he let it grow wild? In any case, she had no intention of being here to see it. She might go back to Bar Harbor, maybe take a cruise—that would make her mother happy.

Jack was speaking, his voice low and strained.

Although she tried not to hear him making excuses, like little poison arrows, his words washed over her. "Last night was a mistake." He'd said that earlier. How many times did he have to repeat it before it sank in?

She sighed. "Yes."

"We need to make a decision."

"I don't know what you mean."

"You could be pregnant."

Abby felt her face flush with humiliation. "I don't think so."

"But you can't be sure," he pointed out with a deep frown. "We can't take that chance. We should get married. We shared a bed, made love. Drew's a friend, I could never face him again."

He was proposing—as in marriage!

Because of his loyalty to Drew!

If the matter weren't so serious, she would have burst out laughing. As it was, she wanted to cry. Abby couldn't believe what she was hearing. But the words he didn't say were the words that mattered most.

"What about love?" she asked, latching on to a small piece of sanity.

Jack looked uncomfortable. Obviously, he had no intention of letting himself love her. "What about it?"

Just as Abby feared, his proposal was based on a misplaced sense of honor. He was playing it safe, guarding his heart from invasion, using a possible pregnancy as an excuse to propose. No matter how tempted to accept his proposal on any terms and worry about the consequences later, Abby simply couldn't pretend his indifference would one day turn to love.

"Thanks for the offer." Understanding him better than he could possibly know, Abby went to him. Ignoring his wary expression, she leaned close, wrapped her arms around his hard waist and kissed him very gently on the mouth.

Despite the warmth of her kiss, Jack began to worry. Why did it feel like good-bye?

"But I can't accept." She slowly stepped back—out of his reach. "Besides, you're not under any obligation to marry me, Jack. You see, it isn't necessary."

She was turning him down!

His mouth tightened. "I think it is."

She shook her head. "No."

"Why not?" He swallowed his disappointment.

So, he'd been right about Abby from the beginning—she didn't love him. Thank goodness he hadn't actually broken down, done the unthinkable and confessed he loved her!

Wait a minute. Could that be what was missing? What if he actually said the words? What if it was true? What if he loved Abby? What did he know about love? Not a thing.

Abby took a deep breath. With her face flushed, she said softly, "Last night, you never asked if I was a virgin."

"I assumed you and Seth had—"

"We didn't." She stopped him cold. "You see, I spent years waiting for Seth. Then I discovered he was the wrong man."

"Abby—" Jack held his breath as he waited for her to say it, and yet he didn't want to hear the words. Because if she told him she loved him one more time, he was going to have to do something about her.

"I like Seth, but he isn't you," she said softly. "I love you, Jack. It's a shame you'll never know how much, because about last night—"

He braced himself. "What about it?"

"You blacked out from the painkillers. We never made love. So, you see, I couldn't possibly be pregnant. There's no necessity for this grand gesture. You're free. You don't have to marry me."

His heart froze. He was free, that meant she was free as well. "I'm sorry it has to end this way. An accident of fate threw us together, but that doesn't mean I belong in your world."

Her eyes flashed at the words. "I don't belong there either, I belong with you. That's the only place I want to be. I'm sorry you can't accept that."

He smiled with wry admiration. "You are one tough lady."

"I don't know what you mean."

Jack struggled to come up with an answer to satisfy

her. After so many false starts and misunderstandings, he had to find the right words—words he'd never said to a living soul. Without them, Abby was leaving. This time, it was final. He knew exactly where he wanted Abby. In his bed, in his house, in his heart. She filled every empty space. Now if he could only convince her.

The next move was up to him. All right—better to give in gracefully than suffer a lifetime of deprivation. Face it. Abby meant everything to him. She was the future, the only reason he'd fought so hard to recover. He'd thought it was to free her—but now he knew better. In the end, what did a man like him have to offer a woman like Abby Pierce? Not a thing. Just himself. Was that enough?

It would damn well have to be because he wasn't about to let her go. With that decision, Jack released a slow breath, then started toward her—his steps slow and unsteady—as if he was just learning how to walk. And maybe he was.

"You never give up, do you?"

"You're wrong." She laughed shakily. "I'm leaving. I'm going back to Bar Harbor. Just as soon as I can pack my things and—"

"No, you're not." He dropped his crutches, reached out and drew her into his arms. There was only one way to silence her; he kissed her. Time spun out before he let her draw a breath. "I think we should stop pretending and just get married for all the usual reasons."

"Such as?"

"I love you." The words had to be choked out.

Her eyes darkened. "How can I believe you aren't doing it for Drew, or because people will gossip, or—"

A slow smile started in his eyes. "This is as real as it gets, Abby. I want forever with you, I want to go to bed and wake up beside you every day for the rest of my life."

Abby frowned. "Are you sure?"

"I'm sure." Holding her close, he leaned against the porch rail, praying she wouldn't resist because he was feeling just a little unsteady. Would fate be kind after a lifetime of trials and bitter disappointments? "Abby, you are the one and only love of my life. Will you marry me?"

"Then, the answer is yes." With the sun shining in her eyes, and the future a fragile dream in her heart, Abby promised him forever.

A man didn't get too many second chances in life. But Jack got his. Before he kissed her, he smiled, a little dazed but happy and content, feelings he intended to explore further. "For as long as I live, I will never know why you climbed that mountain, then got on that rescue helicopter."

Abby smiled that bewitching *Miss Abigail* smile that always had him running for cover, but now he stood his ground and simply smiled back at her. She wrapped her arms around him as if she'd never let go. He prayed she never would because he intended to hold her to his last breath.

"That was the easy part," she whispered, a soft sweet breath of surrender against his lips. "I followed my heart."

Epilogue

Six months later.

Jack and Abby had wanted a small intimate wedding, but her mother had had other ideas. Deciding it might be diplomatic to agree with Myra's plans, they'd given her free rein with the arrangements.

The weather cooperated with a perfect early-September day. Baskets of lush gold and russet flower arrangements and white satin bows lined the steps to the church. All was perfection. Nevertheless, the wedding got off to an awkward start. Jack didn't have any family, and half of Abby's family wasn't speaking to the other half.

Caught in the middle of the family feud, Abby stood outside the small white-steepled church. She regretted giving in to her mother's insistence on a big formal wedding. Her entire family—with the exception of her youngest brother Cal who hadn't arrived yet—stood around waiting for someone to make the first move. The organ swelled again—that was her cue. Abby released a sigh of relief when Drew took the initiative and broke the ice.

With Olivia and their new baby girl tucked under one arm, he crossed the walk, kissed his mother and shook hands with his father.

"Mom, Dad." Once branded the black sheep of the family, deservedly so, Drew introduced his wife, Olivia, "—and this is Elizabeth."

Barely a month old, the cherubic, fair-haired infant looked exactly like her mother. Elizabeth represented the union of two proud families, the Pierces and the Carlisles.

At the sight of her first grandchild, Myra's face crumpled. "May I hold her?" She took the baby and turned to her husband. "Sam, look how precious."

Abby's father cleared his throat. "Congratulations." There was an emotionally charged pause before he added, "—son. I heard the sawmill is busy."

Drew nodded. "How about a grand tour later?"

Sam nodded. "I'd like that." The organ groaned, announcing that the start of the ceremony was imminent. "Well, I guess we should get moving."

Abby took her father's arm. "You sure you know what you're doing?" he said. "There's still time to call the whole thing off."

Abby smiled serenely. "I'm sure."

"Good girl." Sam Pierce grew serious. "Don't ever let pride come between you and those you love."

"You're here now, Dad. That's all that matters."

He chuckled. "When did you get so smart?"

Abby just smiled, but she knew the exact moment. Jack's accident had changed her life, and his. Like fate, a hand had reached out to help her board a helicopter, and she'd accepted the challenge. And all because of a promise. Now, Jack was waiting for her.

Inside the church, Jack cooled his heels.

He was a wreck.

He'd never worn a tuxedo in his life!

He tugged at the collar, feeling it tighten.

And where was his best man?

The organ started. Jack's heart started to pound like a drum roll. He breathed a sigh of relief when Drew came up to join him at the altar. Next came the attendants dressed in emerald green. And then came Abby.

Jack's eyes feasted on his bride dressed in an elaborate wedding gown. It was lace, off the shoulder with yards and yards of fabric, the most romantic dress he'd ever seen. Abby looked like a princess. He'd never dreamed she could be his. It came to him that despite all their differences, Abby loved him unconditionally, probably more than he deserved. She'd loved him when he was at his absolute worst, bound to a wheelchair, with his entire future uncertain. Yes, she'd loved him even then. He felt deeply humbled.

When Abby's father handed her over, Jack took her

hand, lacing their fingers together. They hadn't re-hearsed that part, but he didn't let go.

Abby took a deep breath to steady her nerves. Jack looked like a stranger—a bridegroom—until he smiled. He looked rakish and dangerous, but she knew he had one weak spot reserved for her.

One more promise.

Though he still walked with a limp, Jack stood straight and tall at her side, his eyes holding hers with a distinct gleam of possession. They exchanged rings and repeated solemn vows. "...to love, honor, and cherish—in sickness and in health." They'd already done that part.

At some point, Abby became aware of a late arri-val, her brother Cal. Now everyone she loved was here under one roof.

When Jack slipped his grandmother's ring on her finger—a gold band graced with one perfect diamond, a circle of love with no beginning and no end—Abby knew she'd come home.

Later, at the reception, there was music for dancing. To Jack's relief, the first dance was a slow waltz.

Smiling ruefully, he drew Abby into arms. "I'm not sure I remember how to do this."

His steps were hesitant at first, and there was that one moment when he had to lean on Abby, but they slowly waltzed around the room, each step measured and sure, bound in love's enchantment—proof that when all else fails, love heals.

"You're beautiful," he whispered against her ear, sending a shiver of anticipation down her spine.

"So are you."

Jack Slade blushed. "Abby, I probably don't deserve you, but I—"

Abby didn't want humility from him. "I love you," she whispered, overcome with emotion.

"I love you back. I have no idea why I'm up here with you today. I'm the luckiest guy in the world. I just haven't figured out why you chose me."

Unshed tears glistened in her eyes. "Oh, Jack, don't you know?" When he looked puzzled, she said, "How could I *not* fall in love with you? You're my hero."

Jack drew her close to his heart. It was uncharted territory, but Abby had proven more than once that she was up to the test. "No, my darling, you are my hero. You saved me. If it wasn't for you, I wouldn't be alive today."

Jack kissed her very, very gently. Thanks to Abby, he'd gotten his second chance at life. It all came true...every dream, every promise.

A cactus blooms in the dark.

And miracles happen.

* * * * *

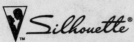
SPECIAL EDITION®

COMING NEXT MONTH

#1537 THE RELUCTANT PRINCESS—Christine Rimmer
Viking Brides
Viking warrior Hauk FitzWyborn had orders from the king: bring back his long-lost daughter. Well, kindergarten teacher Elli Thorson wouldn't be *ordered* to do anything by anyone, handsome warrior or not. But Hauk intended to fulfill his duty and protect the headstrong princess, even if that meant ignoring their fierce attraction to each other....

#1538 FAITH, HOPE AND FAMILY—Gina Wilkins
The McClouds of Mississippi
When the safety of Deborah McCloud's family was threatened, Officer Dylan Smith was there to offer protection. But old wants and old hurts seemed to surface every time the one-time loves were together. Could their rekindled passion help them overcome their past and give them hope for a future—together?

#1539 MIDNIGHT CRAVINGS—Elizabeth Harbison
Chief of Police Dan Duvall was a small-town man with simple needs. So, why was it that city slicker Josephine Ross could stir passions in him he didn't know existed?

#1540 ALMOST PERFECT—Judy Duarte
Readers' Ring
A commitment-phobic ex-rodeo rider like Jake Meredith could *not* be the perfect man for a doctor, especially not an elegant Boston pediatrician like Maggie Templeton—not even when he was her best friend. But when Maggie's well-ordered life fell apart, could she resist Jake's offer to pick up the pieces...together?

#1541 THE UNEXPECTED WEDDING GUEST—Patricia McLinn
Max Trevetti could *not* be having these intense feelings for Suz Grant.... She was his sister's best friend! But Suz was no little girl anymore; their escalating passions seemed to prove that. Would Max and Suz turn away from their desire, or risk everything for love?

#1542 SUBSTITUTE DADDY—Kate Welsh
Brett Costain was just as faithless as his father...wasn't he? That's what he'd been told his whole life. But sweet, small-town girl Melissa Abell made him almost believe he could be husband material—and even a father to her baby—as long as he could convince *her* to be his wife!

SSE